Even unconscious he looked dangerous.

His rich brown hair was short, with an almost military cut. His muscles were powerful, his body as much a weapon as any firearm he might carry.

And everything the man owned fit into two duffel bags.

A husbandless suburban mom, Cindy Jones was willing to admit that this battle-scarred bodyguard sprawled helplessly on her bed was handsome.

But he was also lethal.

Not just because he knew how to kill.

But because he knew how to leave.

And Cindy had learned the hard way that men who left were the most dangerous of all.

Dear Reader,

Silhouette Special Edition welcomes you to a new year filled with romance! Our Celebration 1000! continues in 1996, and where better to begin the new year than with Debbie Macomber's *Just Married*. Marriage and a baby await a mercenary in the latest tale from this bestselling author.

Next we have our HOLIDAY ELOPEMENTS title for the month, Lisa Jackson's *New Year's Daddy*, where a widowed single mom and a single dad benefit from a little matchmaking. Concluding this month is MORGAN'S MERCENARIES: LOVE AND DANGER. Lindsay McKenna brings her newest series to a close with *Morgan's Marriage*.

But wait, there's more—other favorites making an appearance in January include *Cody's Fiancée*, the latest in THE FAMILY WAY series from Gina Ferris Wilkins. And Sherryl Woods's book, *Natural Born Daddy*, is part of her brand-new series called AND BABY MAKES THREE, about the Adams men of Texas. Finally this month, don't miss a wonderful opposites-attract story from Susan Mallery, *The Bodyguard & Ms. Jones*.

Hope this New Year shapes up to be the best year ever! Enjoy this book and all the books to come!

Sincerely,

Tara Gavin
Senior Editor

Please address questions and book requests to:
Silhouette Reader Service
U.S.: 3010 Walden Ave., P.O. Box 1325, Buffalo, NY 14269
Canadian: P.O. Box 609, Fort Erie, Ont. L2A 5X3

SUSAN MALLERY

THE BODYGUARD & MS. JONES

Silhouette®

SPECIAL EDITION®

Published by Silhouette Books
America's Publisher of Contemporary Romance

To Christina Dodd—with thanks for teaching me to survive the wilds of Houston, for explaining that I really do need to unplug my computer during a bad thunderstorm and for generally being a wonderful friend. Here's to incredible success!

SILHOUETTE BOOKS

ISBN 0-373-24008-2

THE BODYGUARD & MS. JONES

SUSAN MALLERY

makes her home in the Lone Star state, where the people are charming and the weather is always interesting. She lives with her hero-material husband and her attractive but not very bright cats. When she's not hard at work writing romance novels, she can be found exploring the wilds of Texas and shopping for the perfect pair of cowboy boots. Susan writes historical romances under the name Susan Macias. You may write her directly at P.O. Box 1828, Sugar Land, TX 77487.

Dear Reader,

I'm thrilled to be part of Silhouette Special Edition's 1000th-book celebration. I'm a relatively new author, and it's an honor to be included with so many of *my* favorite authors.

Silhouette Special Edition books have always been among my favorites. They have provided me with hours of reading pleasure. Now, as a writer, I get to return the favor and do my best to provide you with the same kind of heartwarming, romantic stories that live on far past the last page of the book.

Writing for Silhouette is a dream come true. I'd like to take this unique opportunity to thank three special people for helping turn fantasy into reality. First, Tara Gavin, senior editor of the line. Tara is the talented lady with the vision of what Special Edition books should be. Second, my editor, Karen Richman. Karen encourages me, puts up with me and is the best editor any author could ask for. Finally, I'd like to thank you, the reader. You're the one who loves my hero as much as I do, who roots for my heroine and laughs at my jokes. You're the best part of writing.

Happy reading,

Susan Mallery

Chapter One

"Mister. Mister! Are you dead?"

The voice was insistent and faintly whiny. Mike Blackburne tried to block out the noise, along with the pounding in his head and the painful throbbing that pulsed through his body. He failed miserably on both counts.

"I think he's dead," the voice proclaimed.

"He's not dead. He's sleeping."

"No way. I can't wake him up. See?"

Mike felt a jab in his side. The poking continued, hitting right above the bruise on his ribs. The pain increased, and the black haze he'd been fighting for God knows how long began to descend.

"Leave me the hell alone," he roared. Or at least it was supposed to be a roar. Instead, his mouth barely opened and he mumbled something that sounded like "Ve m'll own."

There was a moment of blissful silence. The jabbing against his ribs stopped. Then his peace was shattered by a high-pitched call.

"Mo-om, he's not dead."

Whatever he was lying on shook slightly, as if it had been bumped. There were footsteps, then silence again.

Mike told himself to sit up. The pain flowing through his body like liquid torture warned him that wasn't advisable. Trying for a lesser goal, he started to open his eyes. His lids felt as if they'd been glued shut.

He tried again and this time was rewarded by a sharp stab of light. He blinked, attempting to bring something, anything, into focus, then wished he hadn't. Some ugly green creature with flaming eyes was staring at him.

He jerked back, causing his head to swim and the cadence of agony to increase. He felt like roadkill. Blinking again, he studied his guardian.

"Hell," he muttered. It was a two-foot-long statue of a dragon, about the ugliest piece of art he'd ever seen. It was just as well he wasn't dead, because he expected the good Lord to have better taste than that.

One corner of his mouth curved up, pulling at his split lip. He grimaced and raised his hand to touch the spot. Tender but not bleeding. Besides, who was he to assume that on his death he was going north?

Footsteps caught his attention. He tried to turn toward the sound. He could see a massive marble fireplace, wing chairs that looked more decorative than comfortable and a small lacquered table supporting a smaller version of the dragon staring down at him. However, he couldn't locate the owner of the footsteps. He hoped it wasn't that kid again. He was in bad enough shape without being poked and prodded.

His eyes closed involuntarily. He didn't want to sleep anymore. He didn't know how long he'd been out. He didn't even know where he was, although something about the room was familiar.

"Mr. Blackburne?"

Soft, sweet tones recalled him to consciousness. She didn't sound like any nurse he'd ever met. But then, he wasn't still in the hospital. Maybe she knew where he was and what he was doing here.

He forced his eyes opened. As everything swam around, he felt a cool touch on his forehead. He blinked.

Directly in front of him were a pair of long, curvy legs. Her honey-colored thighs were about two feet from his face. He could see the bare skin, a freckle above her right knee and a faded scar, probably from some run-in she'd had years before with a curb.

"Mr. Blackburne?" she repeated.

Did angels go around naked? He raised his gaze slightly, hoping to encounter more bare skin. Much to his disappointment, she was wearing pale blue shorts with a white gauzy shirt tucked into the waistband. Leaning over him the way she was, her shirt gaped slightly. He saw the curve of her breasts. A weak but nearly audible flicker of male interest told him he was not only alive, but more than likely on the road to recovery.

Before he could move his head back far enough to see her face, she moved closer and sat next to him. The action took her legs out of his range of vision, but now he could see her features without straining.

She had shoulder-length light brown hair with a fringe of bangs falling to her eyebrows. Her mouth was wide and turned up at the corners, as if she was on the verge of smiling. Her eyes were green, with a hint of gray smoke. He'd never seen her before.

"I hope you feel better than you look, Mr. Blackburne, because you look pretty bad."

"Where am I?" he mumbled. The words came out garbled.

She frowned, a faint line appearing on her forehead. "I can't understand you, but you probably shouldn't be talking, anyway. My name is Cindy Jones. Your sister, Grace, is my neighbor. You're in Grace's house now. You arrived sometime last night, but I wasn't expecting you for another week. If you hadn't left the front door open, no one would have known you were here."

She touched his face again. Her fingertips were cool as she traced a line from his temple to the corner of his mouth. "You've got a fever, and you're bleeding. I don't think you should have left the hospital."

"Hate hospitals."

"Now you sound like Jonathan." He must have looked confused. She smiled. Her lips parted and curved up, exposing white teeth and a dimple in her right cheek. "Jonathan is my oldest. He's nine. He hates anything to do with the doctor. Last summer he broke his arm. You should have heard him complaining every time we took him in to be checked."

Now he knew where he was. He didn't remember much about getting here, although the faint memory of a plane trip made sense. Last time he recalled being fully conscious, he'd been in a hospital in Los Angeles. Grace lived outside of Houston. Why had he gone there? He had his own place....

"Earthquake," he mumbled.

That damn earthquake a couple years back had destroyed his apartment building. He'd meant to find another place, but he'd been too busy working. The memories were coming back faster now. Grace had come to see him in the hospital and had offered her place. She was going to be gone for the summer, anyway. He could recover in peace.

"So who are you?" he asked.

"I told you. I'm Cindy Jones. Your neighbor. Grace asked me to look after you until you were on your feet."

"I don't need any help." He would be fine. As soon as the pounding in his head subsided to a tolerable level and the bullet wound in his leg stopped throbbing in time with his heartbeat. So much for his recovery. "I feel like I was run over by a train."

"Actually, I believe you fell off of a building."

He must have glared at her because she quickly added, "According to Grace, it was a very small building. Some bushes broke the fall."

"They should have done a better job." He concentrated all his strength on getting upright. If he could just swallow a handful of pills that his doctor had prescribed, he would be fine. But first he had to sit up.

He braced his left hand on the sofa cushion and pushed with all his strength. He got about halfway toward sitting before the room started spinning and the shaking in his arm got so bad he collapsed.

"What are you trying to do, Mr. Blackburne?"

"Sit up." He could feel the sweat on his face and back. He hoped it was from the exertion and not a fever. That was the last thing he needed right now.

"Why?"

"Pills." He motioned to the floor, knowing he would have dropped his duffel bags on his way in. His eyelids were getting heavier.

She stood up. He heard her faint footsteps as she crossed the room. There was barely any sound on the hardwood floor, so she must be wearing soft-soled shoes, he thought. A useless piece of information provided by a brain trained to keep him alive. Sometimes, knowing the kind of shoes someone was wearing could save a life. Good to know he still had it, even though he didn't have the strength to use it.

"Is this all your luggage, Mr. Blackburne?" Cindy asked.

"Mike," he mumbled. Everything he owned in the world fit into two duffel bags. If the flight wasn't full, he didn't bother to check them. That way, he could carry them off the plane and not have to wait.

He heard the rattle of pills and knew she'd found the bottles. But instead of handing them to him, she crossed the room toward what he supposed was the kitchen. "Jonathan, keep an eye on Mr. Blackburne. I want to call his doctor."

Mike opened his mouth to tell her not to bother, but no sound came out. Seconds later something poked his injured side. He groaned.

"You really shot?" a voice asked. "Did somebody fill you with lead?"

He forced his eyes open and glanced at the boy staring down at him. He had blond hair, long on top, but trimmed short around his ears. Bright brown eyes peered at him curiously. "Go 'way," he said.

"Can I see the bullet hole? Did you bleed a lot?" The boy looked over his shoulder toward the kitchen, then bent toward Mike's face. "Are you packing a gun?"

Too much TV, Mike thought.

Cindy returned to the living room. From the look on her face, she wasn't happy.

"I spoke to your doctor," she said, holding out a bottle of pills. "He said you were supposed to stay in the hospital another four days. You could spike a fever or worse.''

"Uh-uh. I'm fine."

"You don't look fine. You look like—"

"Garbage?" Jonathan offered helpfully.

"Jonathan."

The boy's shoulders dropped. "Sorry, Mom."

She shoved the pills into her shorts pocket. "Go check on your sister. I'll be home in a few minutes, as soon as I figure out what to do with Mr. Blackburne."

He was having trouble concentrating on what she was saying. "Mike," he told her again. "Call me Mike." At least that's what he thought he said. He had a feeling the words that passed his lips bordered on unintelligible.

"Mike," she repeated. "You shouldn't have left the hospital. I'm not sure what to do with you. We've got a great facility here. I could take you there."

He shook his head. Instantly, black spots appeared. He closed his eyes and rubbed them, but the spots didn't go away. He cleared his throat and spoke slowly, more for his benefit than hers. "I'll be fine. Just get me a glass of water, and I'll take my pills."

"I can't do that."

"Why not?"

"I promised your sister I would take care of you while she was gone. I can't just give you pills and leave you here. You need medical attention. At the very least, you need to be watched. The nurse on the phone said you'd hit your head."

"Listen, lady, I don't need anything but a damn glass of water." He got the whole sentence out clearly.

"Uh-huh. Sorry, but I'm not impressed by your temper."

"Why not?"

She smiled. As smiles went, it was a nice one, he thought, then knew for sure that a fever had kicked in. When did he bother noticing a woman's smile?

"I've got two kids, Mike. I'm used to crankiness in the sickroom."

"I'm not cranky."

"You're doing a fair imitation. I'll make you a deal. If you're strong enough to walk to the bedroom so you can lie down properly, I won't make you go to the hospital."

"Fair enough." He thought about sitting up and wondered if he could do it. "Where's the bedroom?"

"Lucky for you, it's downstairs."

"No problem. Give me a minute."

He concentrated all his attention on his arms, willing them to be strong. After taking three deep breaths, he pushed himself into a sitting position. The room tilted and spun, but he didn't dare close his eyes. Focusing on Cindy, who seemed to be moving slightly less than everything else, he began to rise. His thighs trembled, his knees refused to lock and he felt himself start to go down. At the last moment, he ducked left. The last thing he needed was to be impaled on that damn ceramic dragon.

Cindy thought Mike might actually make it to his feet. He was almost there, when he started to topple like a half-assembled tower from one of Jonathan's games. She lunged forward, catching him before he fell. She grabbed him around the waist. His left arm encircled her shoulder.

It didn't do any good. He outweighed her by about sixty pounds, and he was unconscious. It was like trying to hold up a large, male sack of flour. Her legs buckled, and she found herself pinned under him on the sofa.

His head rested on her chest, his right hand slipped between her thighs. His torso settled across her hips. She couldn't move. The intimacy was almost as unsettling as the heat she felt from him. He had a fever.

"Mike?" she said.

He didn't budge.

"Mike?" She shook him. Nothing. Not even a hint that he could hear her.

A strand of hair settled on her face. She blew it away and studied the situation. Her left foot barely touched the ground. If she could push off with that leg, she might be able to roll him a little and slide out from under him. Her right arm was caught between him and the sofa; her right leg bent awkwardly and was likewise captured.

She glanced at the dragon resting on the glass coffee table in front of the sofa. "You could help," she said.

The dragon didn't answer.

Cindy pushed and wiggled and only succeeded in pulling her shirt out of her waistband and bunching her shorts up around her rear.

"I'm not making progress here," she said, then giggled. Who exactly was she talking to?

"Jonathan?" she called as loudly as she could. "Allison? Mommy needs your help."

She figured the odds of her children hearing her were slim, but she had to try. She wasn't sure how long they would wait before coming to investigate. If they got interested in a show on TV, it could be an hour or more.

"I can't wait that long," Cindy said. She wiggled to get free, and instead managed to wedge Mike's hand tighter between her thighs. "If you knew how long it's been since a man touched me there." She giggled again. She had been reduced to talking to inanimate objects and unconscious men. "At least they're not talking back. I do still have a slender hold on my sanity."

The giggle turned into laughter. She again tried to push Mike off her, but she didn't have any strength. She laughed until tears trickled down her temples and into her hair.

"I never have my camera with me when I should."

Cindy turned toward the voice and saw Beth standing in the foyer. "Help me," she said.

Beth raised her eyebrows as she took in the scene before her. "I understand about getting them a drink to relax them, but Cindy, honey, I think you went too far. And, if you're going to have sex with a stranger, try to remember to close the front door."

"But if he's not a stranger, I can leave the door open?" Cindy shoved against Mike, but he didn't budge. "Would you help me, please?"

Her friend sauntered across the room. She was slim, with dark red hair and brilliant blue eyes. She bent close. "He's handsome. Does he have a name?"

"Mike Blackburne. Grace's brother."

"Oh, my. The bodyguard. Very nice. Grace didn't mention he was so good-looking. I like that in a man."

"Beth! I can't breathe here."

"Stop whining. I'm going to help." Beth grabbed him by the shoulder and raised him slightly. At the same time, Cindy pushed off and managed to slide out from under him. She shimmied off the sofa and plopped onto the floor on her backside.

"He was so overcome by lust that he passed out?" Beth asked.

"I think it was the fever. He's sick."

"Most men are."

Cindy shook her head. "No, I mean he's ill. Grace told me he'd been shot and fell off a building. I spoke to his doctor's office. He left the hospital too early. His doctor said he needs to take his medication and rest."

Beth eyed him. "If you ask me, he needs a new line of work."

"Help me get him to bed."

"You're going to keep him?"

"He's not a puppy. I can't send him back where he came from."

"Take him to the hospital."

Cindy looked at the unconscious man sprawled out on the sofa. The doctor had given her instructions on how to care for Mike. As long as she got his pills and some water down him, all he really needed was a little rest. He sure hadn't wanted to go back to the hospital and she couldn't blame him.

"I promised Grace I would look after him while he was here," she said. "I owe her."

"I'm sure she didn't expect her brother to be so ill."

"Probably not," Cindy agreed. "But she's already gone. I want to try and take care of Mike. If he gets worse, then I'll take him over to the hospital."

"Mike?" Beth raised her eyebrows. "You two have met?"

"Yes, before he passed out."

"And is there a Mrs. Mike?"

"I didn't ask." Cindy stood up and brushed off her shorts. "Don't start matchmaking, Beth. I mean it. Mike Blackburne is a professional bodyguard. He goes from job to job. He's here because he doesn't have a place of his own. I'm not interested in a man like that, and he wouldn't be interested in me."

"I'm not saying you have to marry him," Beth said, tilting her head so she could study Mike's features more clearly. "I'm just saying that once he's on his feet, maybe the two of you could—"

Cindy cut her off. "I'm not that type."

Beth smiled slowly. "Honey, we're *all* that type. It's just that some of us get a little more of a chance to prove it than others."

"Cheap talk for a woman who's been married to the same man for fifteen years."

"I know, but a girl can dream." She touched Mike's cheek with the back of her hand. "He's burning up. If you're serious about taking care of him, there's no point in putting him in Grace's bedroom. You'll just have to run back and forth between the two houses. Let me go get Darren and the three of us can wrestle Mike into your place."

"That makes sense," Cindy said. "I'll take his things over."

"Be right back."

Beth left the house and crossed the street to her own place. Cindy heard her calling for her husband. Thank goodness it was Saturday. There was no way she could have moved Mike on her own.

Cindy picked up the two duffel bags on the floor, went out the front door and cut across the green lawn. She walked down the driveway and into her own house through the back door.

"Mommy, Mommy, is he really dead?" seven-year-old Allison asked. "Jonathan says he's dead, but Shelby and I don't believe him."

"He's not dead, but he's sick. He's going to stay with us for a little while."

Jonathan eyed the duffel bags. "You think he's got a gun in there?"

Cindy clamped her lips together. The thought hadn't occurred to her, but Jonathan could be right. "I think the two of you should stay out of the way for the next few minutes. Mr. and Mrs. Davis are going to help me bring Mr. Blackburne over here."

Allison's big green eyes widened. "Where's he going to sleep?"

"In my room. It's downstairs."

"Daddy won't like that."

Cindy didn't bother pointing out that Daddy had given up his right to complain when he'd walked out on his family nearly two years ago.

"Daddy doesn't care about us, stupid," Jonathan said.

"He does care, and I'm not stupid. Shelby says *you're* stupid."

"At least I'm not dumb enough to talk to invisible people."

"She's not invisible. She just doesn't want mean boys like *you* seeing her."

"Children!" Cindy said loudly. "Please. No name-calling. I mean it."

They both looked at her. Cindy raised her gaze toward the ceiling. It was only the first weekend of summer vacation. It was going to be a long three months.

"Sit," she said, pointing to the floral-print sofa in the family room. They both sat.

Cindy picked up the duffel bags, walked through the formal living room and into the master bedroom. After Nelson had moved out, she'd redone her room in cream and rose. The heavy oak furniture he favored had been replaced with bleached pine and lacy curtains. She put down the bags and, working quickly, she pulled back the decorative pillows and comforter, then smoothed the sheets. Thank goodness she'd changed them that morning.

When that was done, she approached the two duffel bags. She hated to go through Mike's things, but Jonathan had a point. She couldn't keep a gun in the house with her children. Mike was a bodyguard. It made sense he might carry a weapon with him. Sending out a mental apology, she unzipped the first bag.

Five minutes later, she knew that Mike Blackburne wore only button-fly jeans, had an eclectic taste in reading material, owned one pair of dress shoes and had a passport that had been stamped by every country she'd ever heard of and several that she hadn't. But he didn't carry a gun.

She exhaled the breath she hadn't known she'd been holding. A week ago, her neighbor Grace had asked her to look after her older brother while he recovered from his injuries. After all Grace had done for her, Cindy was pleased to finally have an opportunity to pay her friend back. At the time, however, she hadn't thought looking after Mike would turn her life upside down.

Beth stuck her head in the room. "Darren's ready, if you are." She pointed to the bed. "Where are you going to sleep?"

"Upstairs in the guest room."

"You are so conventional. As my only single friend, I count on you to allow me to vicariously experience the thrill of the mating game. I must tell you, I've been very disappointed in your performance to date."

Cindy pushed her friend from the room. "I'll try to do better."

"Starting when?"

Cindy ignored her. As they passed her children, she said, "We'll be right back."

When they were outside, Beth leaned close. "Are you going to take his clothes off?"

"I hadn't really thought about it."

"Can I watch?"

"I thought I might ask Darren to do that."

Beth pouted. "And you call yourself a friend."

Cindy led the way into Grace's house. Darren was already raising Mike into a sitting position. Even unconscious he looked dangerous. His brown hair was short, with an almost military cut. His muscles were powerful, his body as much a weapon as any firearm. All he owned fit into two duffel bags. She was willing to admit he might be handsome, but he was also lethal. Not just because he knew how to kill, but because he knew how to leave. Cindy had learned early in life that men who left were the most dangerous of all.

Chapter Two

Mike opened his eyes because he could hear breathing. It was faint but there. In the moment before his vision focused, he wondered what he would see. Maybe a nurse. Certainly a stranger. He wouldn't have been too shocked to see the devil himself. Instead, the person next to him was a child. A little girl.

"'Morning," he said and was pleased that his voice worked.

She wasn't very tall or very old. He didn't know enough about children to guess their ages, but figured this one was more than five and less than ten or eleven. She had short blond hair that was curly on the ends and big green eyes. She wore a ribbon in her hair—a blue one that matched her blue-and-white T-shirt. When she smiled at him, he knew exactly who she was—the daughter of that woman. Cindy Jones. The dimples were identical.

"I'm Allison," she said. Her voice was faintly sing-songy, and high-pitched. If he'd had a hangover, he would have winced at the sound. But surprisingly, the pounding in his head had reduced from a jackhammer pounding to a dull knocking and he was able to ignore it.

"Hi, Allison. I'm Mike."

"Mommy says you're hurt. That we have to be real quiet while you get better. Mommy said you fell off a building. You shouldn't do that."

"Gee, thanks." Advice always came too late to do any good. He glanced around the room. This wasn't his sister's living room, and if his memory was working any better than his body, it wasn't her bedroom, either. "Where am I?"

"Mommy's room." Allison held a doll clutched to her chest. Her green eyes regarded him solemnly. "She had to go to the store, and she asked me to watch you. You've been sleeping."

"You're watching me?"

She nodded. "I've never watched anyone big before."

He wondered if Cindy had meant for her daughter to stand at his side staring. "You seem a little young to be baby-sitting."

Allison dimpled. "I'm seven. Jonathan's watching TV, and Mrs. Davis is watching us. She was here until a minute ago, but she had to go start her dinner. The front door is open and she screams across the street all the time. Mr. Davis has a seizure if his food isn't on the table at six. But he has other 'deeming qualities." She paused to draw in a breath. "Do you know what 'deeming means?"

"Sorry, no." He didn't know what she was talking about. Or why a seven-year-old had been left in charge of him. He also wondered what day it was and how long he'd been out. He'd arrived on Saturday morning. So today was... "It's Sunday, right?" he asked.

Allison shook her head. "Tuesday. You've been asleep for a long time." She tilted her head. "You say bad words in your sleep. And you get all twisted up in the covers. You had a fever, too. Mommy had to take care of you and I was very quiet."

Tuesday? What the hell happened to Sunday and Monday? He couldn't have been asleep that long. He reached up and rubbed the stubble on his face. Only the innocent stare of the child kept him from grinding out another bad word. He'd been out of it for over seventy-two hours. Then he wondered what else he'd said.

"Could I have a glass of water?" he asked.

She smiled. "I'll get it." She placed her doll on the bed and ran out of the room. "He's awake, and he asked *me* to get him a glass of water," he heard her call as she ran through the house.

Footsteps clattered on the hardwood floor. Mike tried to sit up. His body didn't want to cooperate. He compromised, stuffing a couple of pillows behind his head so he could see more. He did a quick survey of the room. It was spacious, maybe twenty feet square, with a big bay window at one end. The walls were a pale pink, trimmed in cream. The light-colored furniture was large, but simply designed so the big pieces appeared more feminine. An armoire sat across from the foot of the bed. A dresser was next to that. Opposite the window was a doorway that led to a bathroom. Beside the door stood a highboy.

Someone approaching the room interrupted his inspection. The footsteps didn't sound like Allison's so he wasn't surprised when a boy entered the room. He was bigger than his sister and looked older. Something tugged at his memory, the faint impression of the boy prodding him into consciousness.

The kid had blond hair like his sister, but brown eyes. The shape of his face was different, as well. He must look like his father. Mike glanced around the room again and wondered if Mr. Jones lived elsewhere.

The boy shoved his hands into his shorts pockets. "Can I see the bullet wound?"

Until that moment, Mike had been able to ignore the pulsing pain radiating from his thigh. The memories crashed in on him. The ambush on the rooftop garden terrace, the madness in the assassin's eyes, the sudden slowing of time as Mike had shoved his client to the ground and pulled out the Beretta he carried with him. The assassin's first round had missed, the second had caught Mike in the thigh. Mike had shot the assassin, and had then been attacked by the man's assistant. In the struggle, Mike had gone off the side of the building. He'd taken the assistant with him. The client escaped unharmed, the bill was paid and Mike was left to move on. Only this time it had been to a hospital instead of another job.

He shook his head to clear it and only succeeded in blurring his vision. The kid was still staring at him expectantly. What did he want? Oh, yeah. To see the bullet wound. "Not right now, sport."

The boy's mouth twisted with disgust. "My name's Jonathan. I just want to look."

Allison entered, carefully carrying a glass of water in both hands. Her pale eyebrows drew together in concentration. When he took the glass from her, she smiled proudly. "I didn't spill any."

"Thanks."

He tried to sit up again, but he didn't have a prayer. The spirit might be willing, but his body was still whimpering and broken. He tilted his head forward and drank the water down in four long swallows.

The liquid was cool and about the best-tasting drink he'd had in weeks. When he was done, he sighed and offered the glass back to Allison. Now both kids were staring at him, their mouths open, their eyes big.

"You drink fast," Allison said.

"I guess," he said, feeling vaguely uncomfortable.

"You ever kill anybody?" Jonathan asked.

Allison grabbed her doll and took a step back. Mike set the empty glass on the nightstand and looked at the boy. "No. My job is to protect people. I'm hired to keep my client safe."

"But someone shot you."

"It happens."

"Was it a bad man?" Allison asked. Her voice was soft and concerned. She continued to keep her distance.

"Yes, he was bad," Mike told her. "He's in jail now. He can't hurt anyone again." For some reason, he wanted to reassure the little girl. He didn't like seeing the fear in her eyes. He tried smiling at her. His lips felt dry and his face was tight. Still, it must have worked, because the wary expression faded and she approached the bed again.

"Shelby thinks you're nice," she said shyly.

"Who's Shelby?" He glanced around searching for yet another kid.

Jonathan rolled his eyes. "Allison, don't be such a baby. Stop talking about Shelby. She's not real."

The girl tightened her grip on her doll. She ignored her brother and leaned closer to Mike. "Shelby's my bestest friend in the world. She doesn't like Jonathan and won't let him see her."

Mike didn't know what to make of this. He was saved from having to answer by the sound of a car pulling up the driveway.

"Mommy's home, Mommy's home." Both kids went flying from the room. Their feet thundered on the wooden floor.

"Stop pushing," Allison ordered.

"Then get out of my way."

"Mo-om, Jonathan's pushing."

"Am not. Quit being such a baby."

"I'm not a baby."

"Are, too! Allie's a baby. Allie's a—"

The voices were abruptly cut off when the back door opened. For the next few minutes, there were only low murmurs, then Mike heard the woman approaching.

She walked into the room and smiled at him. "I'm afraid to ask if you woke up on your own, or if the children are responsible."

"I think it's a little of both."

She bent over the nightstand and pulled open the top drawer. After pulling out a thermometer, she shook it down and placed it under his tongue. She expertly took his pulse, then leaned close and studied his eyes. While she looked at him, he looked at her.

She was as he remembered her. Today she wore a headband to keep her hair off her face, but the color was still light brown and it fell almost to her shoulders. Her eyes were smoky green and the corners of her mouth tilted up. A red T-shirt clung to her breasts. White shorts hugged her hips and exposed long, tanned legs. She didn't look like any nurse he'd ever had, but he wasn't about to complain.

"Your eyes are clear," she said. She touched his forehead, then his cheek with the back of her hand. "You feel cool, too." She removed the thermometer and studied it. "Normal. Finally. So, Mike, how do you feel?"

"Not bad for a guy who fell off a building."

"You've been asleep for three days. According to your doctor, that's exactly what you needed." There was a shuffling at the door. She glanced over her shoulder. "Jonathan, Allison, your ride for swim team will be here in about fifteen minutes. Go get ready."

He heard footsteps on the stairs and the sound of childish voices. "They don't do anything quietly, do they?"

"Not if there's a way to do it loudly." She perched on the edge of the bed. "I can't tell you how relieved I am to have you awake. I've been worried." Her skin was smooth and slightly tanned. When she smiled, there were faint lines around her eyes. He guessed she was close to thirty.

"Are you a nurse?" he asked.

She laughed. The sweet sound caught him off guard, and he felt himself smiling. It was the second time in less than fifteen minutes. Before now, he probably hadn't smiled twice the entire year.

"Hardly. I teach math at the middle school."

"Excuse me for asking, but if you're not a nurse, what the hell are you doing looking after me in your house? This is your house, isn't it?"

She leaned back against the footboard. After drawing one knee up toward her chest, she clasped her hands around her calf. "I'm friends with your sister Grace. She lives next door." She tilted her head. He recognized it as the same move Allison had made. "Grace has lived here four years. If you're her only brother, how come we've never seen you here before?"

"I don't have much time to see family." Grace was always inviting him. And she made him feel that she really wanted to see him. But Mike could never bring himself to visit. He'd always been a loner. It was easier, and in his profession, safer. "You still haven't explained why you didn't just dump me in the hospital."

"I owe her. My kids get out of school about an hour and a half before I get home. Grace looks after them. She won't let me pay her. I can only buy her so many lunches. When her husband found out he would be spending the summer in Hong Kong, she wanted to go with him. Then you got in touch with her. She didn't know what to do. Going to Hong Kong was the opportunity of a lifetime, but you needed a place to recuperate. That's where I came in. I said I would look after you until you were back on your feet."

"Just like that?"

"Of course. She's my friend." She seemed surprised by the question, as if opening her house to a sick stranger was commonplace.

"What does Mr. Jones think about this?"

Her mouth twisted down at one corner. "I didn't consult him. We're divorced."

"I'm sorry."

"It happens. He left me for a trophy wife."

She leaned forward slightly. The movement caused her shorts to gape slightly by her thigh, exposing a hint of white, lacy panties. Mike told himself he was a bastard for looking and forced himself to concentrate on the conversation.

"Trophy wife? You mean a woman he won somewhere?"

"Exactly. A trophy wife is younger, prettier, blonder. Now that Nelson is successful, he wants someone new to share that with. I'm surprised you're not familiar with the phenomenon. It's very prevalent in the suburbs."

"I've never been in the suburbs before."

"You're in for a treat. It's a different world here. One of four-door cars and families. This is the American dream in progress." Her eyes brightened with humor. "I sometimes think I'm the ultimate cliché." She shifted on the bed and sat cross-legged. It made his knees hurt just to look at her. She held up one hand and began counting off on her fingers. "I'm divorced, and I was left for a younger woman. I'm a teacher, a traditionally female profession. I live in a bedroom community, I drive a minivan, I use coupons and I have two-point-four children."

He folded his arms over his chest and grinned. "Let me guess. The point-four child is Shelby, Allison's imaginary friend."

"You've met?"

"She's met me. I wasn't sure where she was standing."

Their gazes locked. Something leaped between them. Something hot and alive—like electricity. Mike felt warm all over, even though he was practically naked under the sheet. His skin prickled and he had the strangest sensation of taking a step off a bridge, or a building. Only this time, instead of falling, he was suspended there.

Cindy's green eyes darkened as her pupils dilated. Her breathing increased. He could hear the rapid cadence in the silent room. His blood quickened and he felt the second flickering spark of desire around her.

Then, as if someone had snapped his fingers to break the spell, it was gone. They both looked away. Mike didn't know if Cindy was feeling the same sense of loss, but he noticed a splotch of color on each of her cheeks.

She cleared her throat. "The only difference between me and most women in my situation is that I got to keep the house. Aunt Bertha, bless her heart, died and left me enough money to pay down the mortgage, pay off Nelson and refinance. You can't keep a place this big on a teacher's salary."

He didn't know what to say, so he blurted out the first thing that came to him. "Why did you marry someone named Nelson?"

She laughed. "It's a question I've asked myself again and again." She leaned forward and lowered her voice. "He wasn't much of a husband. Good riddance."

He tried to remember the last time he talked with a woman. Just talked. Not as a prelude to sex, or because they were working together. Except for his phone calls with Grace, he didn't know that he ever had.

"What about you?" she asked. "Ever married?"

"What makes you think I'm not now?"

"Because you would have gone home to her instead of coming to Grace's."

"Good point. No, I've never been married." It wasn't his style. He didn't believe in getting that close.

"And you've always lived in the city?"

He nodded. "I had a place in New York for a while, then I got a lot of work in Los Angeles. I kept an apartment there until it was damaged by the earthquake a couple years back. Since then I've been working steadily and haven't found anywhere I liked."

She stood up. He couldn't help watching the graceful way she unfolded her legs. He'd dated a couple of models while he was in New York, but he didn't like their bony torsos and straight legs. Cindy's calves and thighs curved as if trying to lead a man astray while tempting him to paradise. He grimaced. He was thinking some strange thoughts. Maybe he'd fallen on his head harder than he'd realized.

"You live a very odd life, Mike Blackburne. You're about to get a crash course on how the other half lives," she said. "Welcome to the world of children and Middle America."

A car honked. She walked to the door and yelled, "Allison, Jonathan, your ride is here."

The two children ran down the stairs and over to her. She bent down and kissed them both. "Be good."

They called back that they would, raced across the floor, then slammed the door shut behind them. Cindy drew in a breath. "Ah, blissful silence. You hungry?"

At her question, his stomach rumbled. "I guess so," he said.

"I'll make you some soup." She glanced over her shoulder. "Think you can manage to get to the rest room on your own?"

He eyed the door. "Yeah."

"I have chicken soup with round noodles, noodles shaped like dinosaurs and alphabet noodles."

"You're kidding."

"Obviously you've never had to feed children."

"I guess not. You don't have any plain flat noodles?"

"Sorry. They're not exciting enough."

She was right. He had entered a strange and different world. "Surprise me."

Cindy set the soup bowl on the tray, shifted the water glass over and stared at the crackers. Dry toast might be better. She hesitated for a moment, then figured the man was unlikely to finish what she'd brought him, as it was. She picked up the tray and headed for the bedroom.

Mike was back in bed but sitting up this time with the sheets and blanket bunched around his waist. His hair had been brushed, although he still needed a shave.

"You look pale," she said.

"I just about had to crawl on the return trip but it was worth it." He pointed to the bowl. "What did you decide?"

"Dinosaurs. I thought they would make you big and strong."

The look he shot her told her he wasn't sure if he believed her or not. She bit back a grin. Better for her if she kept him a little off-balance. Having Mike Blackburne in her house wasn't doing much for *her* equilibrium.

She settled the tray over his lap. The wooden legs held it up off his thighs. "Would you rather have juice than water? I didn't think coffee would be a good idea. You need sleep more than anything, and I don't have any decaf."

"I don't drink decaf," he said, picking up a spoon. "The taste of coffee is bad enough, but at least it has caffeine. If it doesn't keep you up, why bother? Water is fine."

He dipped his spoon into the bowl, then stared at the miniature pasta dinosaurs floating in the chicken broth. After a shrug, as if to say "What the hell," he downed a mouthful.

"Tastes the same," he admitted.

"What did you expect?"

"I'm not sure. Maybe little crunchy bones?"

She smiled. "Tomorrow, when you're stronger."

While he ate, she moved around the room, opening the drapes, then smoothing the folded comforter at the foot of the bed. Anything to keep from staring at Mike. It had been easy to take care of him while he was only semiconscious. She'd awakened him enough to get him to swallow his pills and make him drink water, but they hadn't actually spoken before. Sleeping, he'd been good-looking.

Awake, he was sinfully handsome and dangerously intriguing.

In an odd way, he reminded her of Nelson. The statistics were the same. Both men had brown hair and brown eyes, and were six feet two inches tall. However, that's where the similarity ended. Nelson's face was ordinary. Glasses hid his eyes, which were his best feature. Her ex-husband was pale, slightly flabby, at least he had been the last time she'd seen him naked, and had the beginnings of a bald spot on the top of his head. His chest was furry to the point of making her wonder if his family tree held the evolutionary missing link.

Mike was broad and strong, tanned with rippling muscles that made her wish he never had to put a shirt on again. His smooth skin made her fingers tingle and her palms itch. He had a strong nose and a square chin. He could have used a couple more inches of hair—she wasn't fond of the military cropped cut—but what was there was thick enough to make him the star of a shampoo commercial. Altogether, he was an impressive male specimen and she didn't know what on earth she was going to do with him. Fortunately, except for helping him get well, nothing was required.

"I unpacked a few of your things," she said, pulling open the top drawer of her dresser and taking out shorts and a T-shirt. "I thought you might like to get dressed."

"That would be great. Maybe later."

When she turned around to look at him, he'd already set the spoon down and was leaning against the pillows. He'd finished all the soup and two of the crackers.

"Do you want some more?" she asked.

"No. I'm weaker than I thought."

"You've been through a lot. What with being shot and all."

He rubbed his chin and grimaced. "You got this funny look on your face when you said that."

"Said what?"

"Shot."

"Not many people around here have much experience with that. We don't get a lot of terrorist activity in the suburbs."

"It's not a lot of fun."

"You've got painkillers," she said, walking toward one of the duffel bags. "Do you want one? And please, don't try to be macho and impress me. I've got children, I'm immune."

"Yeah, okay."

She dug around for the pills, then shook one out onto her palm. "You know, I find it fascinating that you travel with so little luggage. Do you have things in storage somewhere?"

He took the pill from her and downed it with a single gulp of water. After wiping the back of his hand across his mouth, he shook his head. "No furniture or anything. I have my work clothes. Suits, shirts, that sort of thing. I dropped them off at a cleaners in L.A. and he keeps them until my next job. But I don't need a whole lot."

"You're just like my dad. He traveled light, too. If something was too much of a bother, he didn't want it around. It was one of the reasons we never had a dog." She leaned against the footboard post and folded her arms over her chest. She knew men like Mike traveled light emotionally as well as physically. "One day his family got to be too much bother, so he left us behind, too."

Mike grimaced. "That's one of the reasons I never married. In my line of work, it's a mistake."

"You never wanted a home life? Something stable, something of your own?"

"Nope." His brown eyes held hers. "Not my style."

In her heart, she knew exactly what Mike's style would be. He had the looks to turn any woman's head. He would seduce her easily, then move on. He seemed nice enough to issue a warning first, but women too often believed they could change a man, maybe even make him want to stay. Cindy knew better.

"My stepfather was just like my dad," she said. "I guess my mom was attracted to the type."

"Where did that leave you?"

"Alone."

"Is that why you're a teacher with two-point-four children?"

"I guess so. I wanted them to have what I never had. A stable home life. Two parents who really cared about them. I was determined to marry someone sensible. Unfortunately, I picked Nelson." She moved closer to him and reached for the tray.

"Better luck next time," he said.

"Right." Next time she was going to do the leaving so it wouldn't hurt so much. "You're looking pretty tired. Why don't you try and get some rest?"

Mike shook his head. "I was going to tell you I'm fine, but I can't keep my eyes open. I appreciate this, Cindy. I'll get out of here tomorrow."

"Don't be foolish." She started walking toward the door. "According to your doctor, you're going to be here for at least another week. You haven't been any trouble. Besides, it's summer vacation. Having you around keeps the kids from being bored."

She turned back to him. Mike was sprawled out on the pillow, already asleep. A short lock of hair fell over his forehead. His tanned torso contrasted with her pale sheets. The bed and linens had been purchased since the divorce, so Mike was the first male to sleep there.

"Ah, Cindy, you live a wild life," she told herself as she walked into the kitchen. "What would the neighbors think if they knew you had a nearly naked man in your bedroom in the middle of the day?"

The way her luck with men ran, Mike was about as good as it was going to get. She was fooling herself when she said she planned to be the one leaving next time. There wasn't going to be a next time. It was so much easier not to get involved at all.

Chapter Three

Cindy looked up when she heard the knock on her back door. Beth waved and turned the knob.

"I came by to say hi," Beth said.

"Sure you did." Cindy added the flour mixture into the wet ingredients and stirred. "You wouldn't be the least bit interested in how Mike is getting along."

Beth stuck her finger in the bowl and scooped out a taste. She licked off the batter. "You make the best peanut butter cookies on the block. You must be adding something I don't know about. And you have to admit, life is certainly more interesting since your young man came to stay with you."

"He's not a young man, he's close to forty. He's also not mine. And to answer the question I see burning in your eyes, yes, last time I checked he was asleep."

Beth grinned. "Oh, goody!" She slipped off her sandals and walked quietly across the floor. "Yesterday he had his sheet all bunched up around his waist. Do you think it's still like that?''

Cindy rolled her eyes. "Beth, he's been up and sort of staggering around since then. I doubt he's in exactly the same pose. While we're on the subject, I'm sure he wouldn't appreciate knowing you come to look at him like he's some animal on exhibit at the zoo."

"Don't be a stick-in-the-mud. How often does a handsome man just fall into our lives? We must take advantage of the situation. Strike while the iron's hot. Seize the day. Begin as—"

"How many more clichés?"

Beth grinned again. "You don't appreciate me, Cindy. And you should. I'm not just a good friend, I'm highly entertaining." She tossed her head, sending her spiked bangs dancing across her forehead, then turned and headed for the bedroom.

It was several minutes before she returned. Cindy had already filled two cookie sheets and stuck them in the oven. She was filling a third when she heard an exaggerated sigh.

"He's incredibly gorgeous."

She glanced up and saw Beth leaning against the doorway to the dining room. She had a hand pressed against her chest. "I swear I got palpitations just looking at him. Feel."

"Thank you, I'd rather not."

Beth walked over to the kitchen table and pulled out a chair. "My Lord, how do you stand it? He's just lying there, naked."

"He's not naked."

Eyebrows nearly as red as her hair raised slightly. "How would you know?"

"I put out clean underwear every morning, and it disappears."

"How disappointing." Beth leaned back in the chair and sighed once more. "Still, it's just you and him alone. Night after night."

"The kids are here," she reminded her friend. "You're trying to make this into something it's not. Mike is Grace's brother. I'm doing this for her, not him. As for him being attractive..." Beth looked at her. Cindy held up her hands in a gesture of surrender. "Okay, I'll admit he's pretty good-looking."

"Good-looking? The man could jump-start a person in a coma."

"Beth!"

"Well, he could! I just wish he'd wake up so I could see his eyes. What color are they?"

"Brown."

"Oh."

Cindy looked up from the cookie batter. "You sound disappointed."

"I was hoping for something more exciting. Gray maybe, or a nice—" She broke off and frowned. "You know, there aren't many colors for eyes to be, are there? Okay, brown."

The timer on the oven beeped. Beth stood up. Like Cindy, she was dressed in shorts and a T-shirt. The Houston summer heat required a minimum of clothing, even in the air-conditioned house.

Beth grabbed the pot holders resting on the counter and took the baked cookies out of the oven. She set them on the cooling racks on the edge of the island, then grabbed the filled pans Cindy had prepared.

Cindy smiled. This was one of the things she liked about where she lived. Being friends with her neighbors and sharing time with them. She, Beth and Grace had canned fruit together, baked pies and even prepared holiday dinners. They ran back and forth when ingredients were low, the days too long or something bad happened in their lives. Both women had been there for her when Nelson had walked out. She would never forget that.

Beth closed the oven, then tossed the pot holders on the counter next to the cooling cookie sheets. She grabbed a spatula, slipped a cookie off and picked it up. "Hot!" she said, bouncing it from hand to hand and blowing. When it was cool enough, she took a bite. Her eyes closed and she smiled. "Perfect." She offered half to Cindy.

Cindy tasted the cookie and had to admit, she had a way with peanut butter. She took the glass of water Beth had filled and sipped. "I miss Grace," she said.

"Tell me about it. I miss her, and I miss my kids." Beth returned to the kitchen table and sat down. "I know, I know. I'm the one who couldn't wait for them to leave. They annoy the hell out of me. I mean, they're practically teenagers. That's their job. When they said they wanted to go to camp I was thrilled. But it's only been a few days and the house is so quiet and boring."

Cindy smiled. "I thought you and Darren were going to plan things for the two of you to do."

"We are. It's kind of fun, actually. But I still miss the kids. I guess this is what the empty nest is like. I'll end up like those old women who keep their children's rooms as shrines. Everything in its place."

"I don't think so."

"Yeah, me neither." Beth looked up and shook her finger. "Don't try to trick me into changing the subject. How's it going with Mike?"

Cindy thought about pretending ignorance, but there was no point. Beth was like a bulldog. Once she got hold of something, she never let go. "It's not going anywhere. I don't want it to go anywhere. He's just a houseguest. Grace's brother, nothing more."

"He's a single, good-looking guy."

"I'm not interested in getting involved with him or anyone."

"We only want you to be happy."

"We?" She didn't like the sound of that. She picked up the last two unused cookie sheets and began scooping dough into neat rows. "You and Darren, or you and Grace? You haven't been trying to set me up, have you?"

Beth's eyes widened with exaggerated innocence. "Set you up how? The man fell off a building, Cindy. As much as I want you to have a date, I wouldn't send a man close to death just to get you alone with him."

"I suppose." But she was going to grill Grace the next time she spoke to her.

"It's been two years." Beth wasn't smiling now. Her blue eyes were dark with concern. "It's time to let go."

Cindy shifted uncomfortably. When the cookies were laid out neatly, she dipped a fork into a small bowl filled with flour and began making crisscross marks. "I have let go," she said. "I don't want Nelson back. In the last few months, I realized I hadn't loved him for a while. Even before the divorce. But I thought we would stay together forever. I thought we would be friends and offer a stable home to our children. Dating is so—" She shuddered. "I don't even want to think about it. I'm not ready."

"What are you waiting for?"

"Inspiration." Cindy smiled.

"Someone to fall into your lap, so to speak?"

"Don't start on Mike again. I barely know the man." She set the fork down and faced her friend. "It's not as easy as you think. Not many men want a woman with children. Even if I was interested, where am I supposed to meet these guys? I work at the middle school. I'm surrounded by kids all day. I love my job, but it doesn't make it easy to socialize. It's not as if I'm going to meet some cute man at the water fountain.''

Beth rested her elbows on the table and cupped her chin in her hands. ''I see your point. No offense, Cindy, but you're not really the bar type.''

''I agree.'' She shuddered again. She'd been to a bar once, with a friend from work. Another single teacher. It had been hideous. ''Check on Allison and Jonathan, will you?''

''Sure.'' Beth leaned toward the window. ''I can see them playing in the yard. It looks like a game that involves far too much running for the time of day.''

Cindy glanced at the clock on the oven. It was nearly two. ''The swim meet is at five. I should probably bring them in to rest for an hour or so.'' She walked to the window and stared out.

Their house was at the end of the cul-de-sac. Beyond that was a wide expanse of grass and trees with a walking path down the center. The greenbelt was the main reason she and Nelson had bought this particular lot when they'd had the house built. It gave the kids a great place to play. The area was quiet and secluded, safe.

''Don't you ever get tired of being alone?'' Beth asked.

''You mean lonely?'' Cindy glanced down at her friend. She shrugged. ''Sure, but I don't want the kids hurt again. It was hard enough for them when their dad left.''

''Maybe they're not the only ones you're scared about. Maybe you're also worried about yourself.''

''I can't deny that. I've been hurt, too. I'm beginning to think it's easier not to try.''

The timer went off. Cindy moved to the oven and pulled out the cookies. She couldn't imagine herself dating. When would she have time? Nelson only took the kids every other weekend. She wanted them to remember their childhood as happy, not a collection of baby-sitters because their mother was too busy trying to have a social life.

"We've had this conversation before," Beth said.

"Yes."

"You're being very stubborn."

"Probably."

"I care about you because you're my friend."

Cindy set two trays in the oven and set the timer again. "I know you do. I also know you're sweet enough to change the subject."

Beth pursed her lips as if she wasn't going to agree, then she nodded. "Just this once. Now we can talk about Mike some more."

Cindy groaned.

"Darren and I are having a barbecue a week from Saturday. You're invited. Bring Mike."

"What if he doesn't want to come?"

"He has to. Everyone wants to meet him. It will be fun. You'll see. Besides, you have to show him around sometime. You can't imagine the phone calls I've been getting."

Actually, Cindy could. She'd gotten a few of her own. Everyone was curious about "Grace's bodyguard brother." "I can't decide if it's the fact that he's single or if it's his career that has everyone so curious," she said.

"It's both." Beth rose to her feet and walked to the refrigerator. "Is it all right?" she asked, motioning to the door.

"I'm sorry. I should have offered. Grab me a soda, too, please."

Beth pulled out two diet sodas. She handed Cindy one, then popped the top on the other. After taking a long drink, she set it on the counter and began sliding cooled cookies into a plastic container.

"Mary Ellen called to find out if I thought she should offer to cook him meals," Beth said.

Cindy snorted. "Yeah, right. Does this mean she's done having her way with the delivery guy?"

"Probably not. But I would say the affair is winding down. You know how she likes to have someone waiting in the wings."

"Mike is in a weakened condition," Cindy said. She finished spooning out the last of the cookie batter and set the bowl in the sink. "I'm going to have to protect him from Mary Ellen. That brunette bombshell could kill a man."

"That's not all," Beth said. She sauntered over to the sink and turned on the hot water. "Everyone is very intrigued by the fact that he's staying here with you."

"What?" Cindy spun around and turned off the faucet. "What's that supposed to mean?"

"Don't get mad at me. I'm not making up the rumors, I'm just telling you. After all, it's been two years since Nelson left and you haven't been on a single date. Now you have a naked man living in your house."

Cindy leaned against the counter and sighed. "He's not naked," she said weakly, then wondered if it really mattered. She knew how people talked in small communities. Gossip spread faster than fire ants. Nothing was as interesting as what everyone else was doing.

"I hope you're telling everyone he's been injured," she said. "My goodness, he can barely walk to the bathroom unescorted. We're not having wild sex. My children live here."

"The sex doesn't have to be wild, if that would help."

Cindy just stared at her.

"Fine. Disappoint all your friends. See if I care." Beth squeezed soap into the large mixing bowl and swished it around. When the water was sudsy, she picked up the measuring spoons and cups and dropped them in. She reached for a dishcloth. "It hasn't even been a week, so I'll forgive you for not having had sex yet. But you have to give me something. Have you at least seen him naked?"

"Beth!"

"Oh, please say you have."

"I can't believe we're having this conversation."

Beth looked at her, then at the dishes. "If you see him naked, will you tell me?"

"I'm not going to see him naked."

"But you have to."

"Why?" Cindy stared at her friend. "You've finally slipped over the edge, haven't you? You've lost your fragile hold on reality."

"Of course not. It's just..." Beth drew in a deep breath. "I met Darren in college. I hadn't dated much in high school and he was the first man I, you know, did it with." A spot of color appeared on her cheeks. "I talk big, but the truth is, I've only been with Darren. I've never even seen another man's..." She cleared her throat. "I just want to know what he looks like."

Beth was up to her wrists in soapy water. Cindy took a step closer and gave her a hug. "You're a terrific friend. I was a virgin when I met Nelson, too. So I haven't seen anyone else naked, either."

"It's just so unfair." Beth glanced at her, blue eyes dancing. "Men see women naked all the time. It's in magazines, in the movies. Maybe we should take advantage of that for the next school fund-raiser. We could hire men to walk around naked. Think of the cover charge to get in. It could be a couple hundred dollars. We could buy a lot of sports equipment with that."

Cindy released Beth and stepped back. "You *are* crazy."

"It's a great idea."

"No."

Beth finished washing the measuring cups and rinsed them. "Can I at least go check and see if Mike really has on underwear?"

"No."

"But if I peel the covers back slowly, he won't even—"

"No! I mean it, Beth."

"You're no fun." She rinsed her hands and grabbed a towel.

"Where are you going?"

"Home."

Cindy walked Beth to the door. "You want some cookies?"

"Save them for Mike. He'll need his strength to survive around here. Don't forget. Next Saturday. Say, six o'clock?"

"I'll ask him, but if he doesn't want to come, I can't make him."

"Of course you can. Bat your eyes. If that doesn't work, try a low-cut T-shirt."

"Sorry, they're all like this." She fingered the neckline of her crewneck shirt.

"So disappointing. If you're not going to be a little more wild, I might have to find another single friend."

Before Cindy could answer, Beth gave her a hug. "Take care of yourself and that hunk of yours."

"I will."

As Beth crossed the street, Cindy glanced around the house toward the greenbelt. About eight children were playing together in the shade of a pecan tree. She wondered where they got their energy. It was about ninety-four degrees and the humidity was nearly that high. Just standing in the open doorway was making her sweat.

She stepped inside and shut it behind her. The timer on the oven dinged.

After taking out the last batch of cookies, she put a couple of cool ones on a plate, then poured a glass of lemonade. A quick glance at the clock told her it was almost time for Mike to wake up. In the last couple of days, they'd settled into a routine. He slept for an hour in the morning, then right after lunch. He spent his afternoons reading or watching TV. Every day he was getting a little stronger, but he wasn't going to be back at work anytime soon.

She carried the plate and glass into the bedroom. He was sitting up against the pillows.

"I thought you'd still be asleep."

"Oh, really? But the conversation you and your friend were having was so interesting."

She started to set the plate down, then froze. Heat burned her cheeks as embarrassment flooded her. "You heard us?" she asked, her voice a squeak.

"I don't know if I heard all of it, but I heard enough." He studied her. "I never knew what women talked about when they were alone. I think it was better that way."

She cleared her throat. After setting the plate and glass on the nightstand, she brushed her hands against her shorts. Her conversation with Beth had been completely innocent, she reminded herself. And private. It wasn't his business.

Except Beth *had* asked about seeing him naked.

Cindy glanced at his bare chest, then raised her gaze higher to his face. He'd shaved that morning, although he hadn't had the strength to stand. She'd had to bring a chair into the bathroom for him. She could see the strong lines of his face and the slight tilt at the corner of his mouth. One eyebrow raised expectantly. She didn't know if he was annoyed or mad.

"It's Friday," she said at last. "If it makes you feel any better, on Monday we generally discuss women being naked. We try to be fair about it."

Mike grinned. Cindy returned his smile, her relief tangible.

"Beth sounds like a scary lady," he said.

"She's really very nice. Oh, did you hear about the barbecue?"

"Just a word here and there." He'd been asleep until a strange woman had tiptoed into his room. Their conversation had carried to him in the quiet house, although when they ran water in the kitchen, it drowned out the sound of their voices.

"Everyone will want to meet you," she said. "You're something of a local celebrity. Not just because you're Grace's brother, but what with your work and the injuries . . ."

He remembered his sister's instructions to be nice to her friends. "I'll go," he said, and knew he would hate everything about the evening.

"It's not until a week from Saturday. I'm sure you'll be better."

"I hope so." He flexed his sore leg and winced.

"I need to change the bandage," she said.

He nodded and flipped back the covers. Cindy went into the bathroom and came back with a small box containing her supplies. She took her nursing very seriously. As he scooted over to give her more room, she settled on the edge of the mattress. He grabbed his leg below the healing bullet wound and raised it while she slipped a towel underneath.

"We're getting to be quite a team," he said.

"Practice." Her hands were small but sure. She gave him a quick, apologetic glance, then carefully removed the bandage.

She studied the hole in his thigh. It was sort of lumpy and still red but it wasn't infected and didn't bleed anymore.

"I think it's better," she told him.

He leaned back as she continued her treatment. Over the smell of disinfectant, he caught the fragrance of her perfume. In the last four days, he'd accepted the fact that she was only ever going to wear shorts and a T-shirt around him and that he'd better get used to long honey-colored legs taunting him at every turn. He wondered how men in the suburbs got anything done with all these half-naked women around. Maybe they became immune, or didn't bother noticing. If so, they were fools.

Having Cindy bend over his injury, with her light brown hair falling loose and her face all scrunched up with concentration, was the best part of his day. Her friend across the street might be all hot to see him naked, but he didn't think Cindy ever noticed he wasn't wearing anything but briefs. To her, he was simply Grace's brother. Almost a eunuch.

Of course, if he kept noticing the way her breasts moved, she would soon have proof he was very much a man. Instead of indulging himself, he forced his thoughts elsewhere. In the last four days he'd learned two things. First, Sugar Land, Texas, wasn't like anywhere he'd ever been before. Even sleeping half the day away, he sensed the difference. Second, Cindy Jones wasn't for him. He might admire her legs, and the way she filled out her shirt, but she was as off-limits as his best friend's wife. If he had a best friend. She'd just admitted she'd only been with one man in her life. He'd never dated anyone for more than a month. He didn't believe in relationships, she needed to be married.

She applied a fresh bandage. "The kids are outside playing," she said and stood up. She reached for the pair of jeans she'd folded earlier and placed on the footboard. "If you can get dressed and out to the family room before they come inside, that means you get to control the TV remote. If you don't, they have the power."

He shuddered at the thought. "Do you know what's in those cartoons?"

"Yes, that's why I try to be out of the room." She tossed him the jeans, then bent over his duffel bag and dug out a T-shirt. "Think of it as your aerobics exercise for the day. A race for the remote control."

His heart was already getting a workout, he thought, watching the way the fabric of her shorts pulled tight around her derriere. The feminine curves tempted him. He didn't know what the problems had been in her marriage, but he was willing to bet her husband hadn't left because he wanted someone better-looking. If Mike was wrong, her husband was a fool.

Cindy tossed him a T-shirt then started for the door. Before she left, she glanced back at him. "About Beth," she said, then nibbled on her lower lip. "She's just talking. She tries to be very worldly and all, but she's in love with her husband. She'd never actually do anything."

"I know."

"I just didn't want you to think that she was like that."

"Maybe when I meet her, I should offer her a quick look."

Cindy laughed. "Only if I can be there to see the expression on her face."

"Deal."

"Get dressed, eat your snack, then head for the family room. The kids will be outside for another half hour or so."

With that, she left. He found it humorous that she would tend to the wound on his thigh but she always left him alone to dress. She treated him with amused tolerance. He couldn't remember the last time he'd joked with someone, or bothered to relax. He'd been working too hard, without a break between jobs.

If nothing else, this forced time off would give him a chance to regroup. As soon as he was able, he could move into Grace's house. Once there, he would think about what it was he wanted to do with his life. His recent encounter with death had him wondering about different career options. He was pushing forty. Next time he might not be so lucky.

He grabbed his jeans and started to slip them on his good leg. Before he'd pulled them up past his knee, there was a scream from outside.

"Mommy, Mommy, Allie's been hurt."

"Allison!"

Mike heard Cindy race through the house, open the front door and call for her daughter. He jerked on the jeans, and about lost his balance when his head started to swim. He grabbed the footboard and held on. The room twirled and darkened, then slowly returned to normal. He pulled the trousers up over his hips and quickly fastened the buttons. He started out the door in a slow shuffling step.

Pain radiated from his bullet wound. Darkness nipped at the edges of his vision. He could hear conversation and someone crying. As he reached the entryway, Cindy came in carrying Allison in her arms.

The little girl was sobbing. She clung to her mother as blood oozed from a scrape on her knee. Behind them, Jonathan and a couple of other kids he didn't know trailed in. Cindy looked up and saw him.

"Mike, could you bring that box of medical supplies into the kitchen, please?" Before he answered, she looked over her shoulder. "Billy and Ashley, you're going to have to go home now. Jonathan, shut the door."

Mike headed for the bathroom. By the time he got to the kitchen, he was breathing hard and hanging on to walls for support. Jonathan stood by the entrance to the family room, just watching. Cindy had settled on one of the kitchen chairs, with Allison's injured leg propped up on the one next to it. Using a damp washcloth to wipe away the dirt, Cindy cleaned the still-bleeding wound.

Mike shuffled forward and placed the first-aid kit on the table. Cindy glanced up at him. Her green eyes widened. "You look like you're going to pass out. Take a seat."

He sank onto the chair across from hers.

Allison's cries had quieted to sniffles, but she still kept her face buried in her mother's neck. She winced as the washcloth touched her scrape.

"Hush, baby girl," Cindy murmured. "It's going to be all right."

She reached for the antiseptic and dampened a cotton ball. Mike flinched, knowing what was coming. He'd treated some bad wounds before, but those had been on adults. This was seven-year-old Allison who came to visit him every morning and told him about her imaginary friend, Shelby. He hated to see her face streaked with tears.

"Take a deep breath," Cindy warned, then touched the cotton to the scrape. Allison shook all over. She sucked in another breath, then let it out in a hiccuped sob.

"I know," her mother told her. "Almost done. You're going to be fine, although I don't think you'll be swimming this afternoon."

"Can I still have cookies?" Allison asked, then sniffed.

"Sure." Cindy opened a bandage and placed it over the scrape. After smoothing it in place, she hugged her daughter close.

Mike stared at the pair. He felt something odd inside. A hollowness, as if he was just now noticing a piece that had been missing from his life for a long time. The ache felt old and bitterly familiar. It came from being on the outside looking in.

As Cindy held her child and rocked her, light brown hair fell over blond. Her voice was soft as she hummed tunelessly. He could hear Allison's breathing calm.

The girl opened her eyes and looked at him. A single tear dripped onto her mother's shoulder.

"Better?" he asked.

Allison nodded.

It was as if a giant fist were squeezing his heart. Maybe it was seeing all he'd never had. Not just the house, although his family had been poor. He'd grown up in a one-bedroom apartment, sleeping on the sofa, or the floor of his mother's room if she was entertaining. He'd always felt passed over in the business of her life. First she'd been working so much, then she'd remarried and had Grace.

Her new child had claimed her time. Funny, he'd never blamed his half sister for that.

Watching Cindy hold Allison reminded him of all he'd missed. The caring, the bond between a mother and child. The love. Until that moment, he'd forgotten the emotion even existed.

Chapter Four

Mike braced his hands against the tiled wall of the shower and let the hot water run over him. He breathed in deeply, noticing it didn't hurt so bad to inhale. Pretty soon he would be able to cough and sneeze like a normal person.

When he'd rinsed the shampoo from his hair, he reached for the bar of soap and lathered it leisurely. As he rubbed the bar over his body, he noted which parts still hurt like hell and which were healing. The bullet wound would take the longest. The entry hole was just about closed, but the exit wound was still nasty looking. In the next day or so, he was going to have to start rehabilitation. As he rinsed off the soap, he grimaced. Rehabilitation was a fancy way of saying he would spend the next three months sweating in a gym, slowly bringing his torn and injured muscles back to normal.

He turned slowly under the spray, then pushed in the knob to turn off the water and stepped out of the shower. The bathroom was large enough that the steam simply floated away. The wide mirror opposite didn't fog up. Instead, it reflected his image clearly. He snapped up the towel he'd left hanging on the hook and ran it over his chest and arms. After passing it over his legs, he rubbed his hair, then wrapped the towel around his waist.

Mike limped toward the double sinks. Cindy had left his shaving kit next to the one on the left, so that's where he brushed his teeth and shaved.

The silence of the house sounded odd on this weekday morning. Usually, one or both of the children were inside playing, running or shrieking. He'd grown used to dozing between the calls of various games or the thunder of feet on the stairs. Cindy tried to keep them quiet when he was resting, but he'd quickly learned that a grown-up's and a child's definition of quiet were extremely different.

He'd had a bad night, with the pain keeping him awake, even after he'd taken his pills. As he bent over the sink and splashed shaving cream off his face, he felt the twinge in his leg. It was better today. He'd been shot before so he knew the drill. There would be bad moments, and good ones. Eventually, it healed and only the weather would remind him of the injury.

This morning, Cindy had taken the children to the grocery store with her. Mike had asked her to pick up a few things for him. He wondered if she was getting tired of nursing him, but every time he mentioned leaving, she insisted he stay until he was more mobile. He didn't mind being here. The kids were kind of fun and Cindy was prettier than any nurse he'd ever had. Between her shorts and those snug T-shirts she wore, he was about ready to—

The sound of the doorbell cut through his thoughts. He finished wiping his face, then limped to the front door. The marble tiles in the entryway were cold on his bare feet. The beveled-glass window in the wooden front door allowed him to see the shape of the person on the other side, but not her features. He turned the lock and pulled open the door.

The woman in front of him was in her sixties. Despite the already rising temperature of the Houston summer morning, she was wearing a long-sleeved dress in a blue-and-green floral print, with a little straw hat on her head. Tight gray curls marched across her forehead. A purse hung over her left forearm and she was clutching a clipboard to her chest.

"Yes?" Mike asked when the woman didn't say anything.

She stared. Her small blue eyes widened and her mouth opened. There wasn't any sound.

"Were you looking for Mrs. Jones?" he asked.

The woman nodded. She was short, maybe an inch over five feet, with the matronly roundness of a grandmother. Her face paled, until the powder she was wearing seemed colorful by comparison.

"Is she here?" the woman asked, her voice high-pitched and shaking. Her gaze, which had swept over him thoroughly, now settled on his bare feet.

"Not right now. She's at the grocery store. I expect her shortly. May I give her a message?"

"And you are?"

He frowned. "A friend."

"I see." With that, she handed him a sheet of paper. At the top, a banner reminded the reader of the annual blood drive at the local church. "If you could give this to her, please."

Mike glanced down at the towel he was wearing and groaned silently. Damn. He was flashing the local church lady.

"Ah, ma'am? Cindy, ah, Mrs. Jones, is a friend of my sister's. I was recently injured on the job and she's been taking care of me. It's not what you think."

The woman turned smartly and started down the walkway, never once looking back. He thought of continuing his explanation, then figured she wouldn't believe him, anyway. He swore again.

Before he could close the door, he heard a call from across the street. As he looked up, he saw a woman standing in her front yard. She had short, dark red hair and the kind of chest that made a man act like a fool.

"Hello," the woman called. "You must be Mike. I'm Beth, Cindy's friend. How are you feeling?"

Beth? The same Beth who had wanted to see him naked? "Fine," he called back.

"I see you're up and around."

And flashing the neighborhood. "Yes. Thanks. See you soon." As he closed the door, he had the fleeting thought that he could solve Beth's problems by dropping the towel, but then figured she would like it too much. As he made his way back to the bedroom, he wondered how he was going to explain the incident with the church lady to Cindy.

By the time Cindy and the kids returned, he'd pulled on jeans and a shirt. He carried in one load of groceries, then had to sit down before his leg gave out.

Allison set a sack of potatoes on the table in front of him and smiled shyly. "Shelby says you're going to get sick again if you do too much."

"Tell Shelby she's a very smart little girl."

Allison dimpled.

"How are you feeling?" Cindy asked as she carried in the last armful of groceries. Jonathan trailed behind her, shutting the doors of the minivan.

"I'm going out to play," he said, hovering by the back door.

"Me, too," Allison added. Her knee was better with only a small bandage covering the worst of the scrape.

"Go ahead," Cindy said, then laughed as they closed the door. "They'll do anything to avoid putting away the groceries. Even play outside in the heat."

"They do that, anyway," he said.

"You're right." She glanced around at the kitchen. "Do you think we have enough food?"

He followed her gaze. The countertops were in the shape of an L. Bags of groceries covered the white surface. There were twelve-packs of soda, cartons of detergent and double packs of cereal.

"Expecting a famine?" he asked.

She chuckled. "It's triple-coupon day. You should have seen the lines. And soda was on sale, along with a great cut of meat. The grocery store does this a couple of times in the summer. I suppose it's to get people out in the heat."

Money was tight. He should have figured that out already. She'd explained that most divorced women couldn't afford to keep their houses. "How much do I owe you for what I've eaten?"

She placed her hands on her hips and glared at him. He supposed she was trying to intimidate him, but all she did was draw her shirt tighter over her breasts. He'd already had two highly erotic dreams about her. He looked away and forced himself to think of something else.

"I was making conversation, not hinting," she said. "I could feed you for a month and not even get close to what your sister has given my kids in snacks and meals. So I don't want to hear another word about paying me for your food.''

"Yes, ma'am." He rose to his feet. "At least let me help put the groceries away."

"Don't be silly. You'll fall flat on your butt." She leaned over the table and pushed on his chest. He was still tired from carrying in two bags, so he didn't argue. He took the glass of juice she offered and watched her put away the food.

She moved around the kitchen with graceful ease. Her movements were almost a dance, the smooth lifting and bending. She kicked off her shoes and he saw she painted her toenails pale pink. Her shorts were red and her T-shirt had a drawing printed on the front that proclaimed her to be Queen of Everything. Small gold hoops dangled from her earlobes and a red headband held her hair off her face.

He supposed there was nothing unusual about Cindy Jones. In this neighborhood, hundreds of women just like her wore T-shirts and bare feet as they put away groceries. Yet, he'd never sat in a kitchen and observed the ritual.

She pulled three pink-paper-wrapped packages out of a bag and sighed. "Pork roast, roasted potatoes and salad. My favorite meal."

"Sounds great."

She placed two of the packages in the freezer and one in the refrigerator, then tossed him the empty bag to fold. "It is. Nelson never appreciated my cooking. He often wanted to go out. But I like eating at home. Which do you prefer?"

Mike was startled by the question. "I don't cook much."

"Of course you wouldn't when you're with a client or subject or whatever you call them. But what about when you're off work? Or did you leave that for your lady friends?"

"Sometimes women cook for me."

She was putting away cereal, raising herself on tiptoe and sliding the new boxes behind the old. As she came down on her heels, she glanced at him and smiled.

"Why is it men can take care of themselves perfectly well when they're alone, but the first second they live with a woman, they suddenly become helpless?" she asked.

"I've never lived with a woman."

The smile faded as her eyebrows drew together. "Really? I knew you hadn't been married, but I just assumed..." Her voice trailed off. She reached into the full bags on the kitchen table and drew out canned beans.

Until she questioned him, he hadn't really thought about it. "My life-style isn't conducive to long-term relationships."

"I guess not." She reached in the bag for more canned goods. "No roommates?"

"I told you I travel light."

"Ah, yes. Extra baggage weighs you down. Fight hard, fight lean." She paused and shrugged. "For a long time I blamed the marines when my father left, but as I grew older, I saw that lots of other officers managed to balance a career and family. They were terrific fathers." She looked in the bags on the table, then picked one up and started folding it. Her green eyes focused on something above his head. "When my father missed an important event at school or forgot my birthday, I used to wish one of the other families would adopt me. My friend Lorraine had a wonderful family. Warm, loving, everything I wanted. I remember thinking it wasn't fair."

Mike was startled when he realized he could picture Cindy as a child. She would look a little like Allison, only her eyes would be dark with pain. "Life's not fair," he said.

"I figured that one out on my own," she said. "Although I still thought I could make it fair when I married Nelson."

She finished folding the bag and slipped it into an open one, then moved to the long counter and started putting away fresh vegetables.

"Why did you get married?" he asked.

"The usual reasons."

"Which are?"

She looked at him over her shoulder. "You don't know?"

"I never married. Never saw the need." Or felt the compulsion. He liked women. Sex was great, but aside from that, he didn't get the point. Why would anyone want to share quarters with someone else? He'd heard the fights, listened to his buddies complain. It was better to be alone. It was certainly easier.

"You ever been in love, Mike?" she asked.

"No." He didn't want to think about the loving part. That was the one piece of the puzzle that eluded him. Without wanting to, he remembered Cindy holding Allison in her arms after the little girl had been injured. The child had clung with the trust of someone who knows they're loved and will be taken care of. Cindy hadn't asked for anything in return, she'd simply given. He believed love existed—he'd seen it. It just didn't live in his world. He hadn't loved anyone, and no one had ever loved him, except maybe his sister.

She leaned against the counter and tilted her head to one side. "It's lovely. Your heart beats fast, your palms get all sweaty."

"Sounds like the flu."

"Funny. When I first met Nelson, I just knew he was the one."

"Because you felt all tingly inside?" The question was meant to come out sarcastic, but instead he sounded curious. And he was.

"Actually, no. That should have been my first clue. With Nelson, the love grew more slowly. I was attracted to him because he was so different from me. His family has lived in Houston for three generations. He was stable. Until college, he'd never been out of the state. I thought he was the answer to my prayers. I was wrong on that one."

"I'm sorry."

"Me, too, but it's done. I'm going to do the best I can with my kids. They're going to have everything I didn't. Stability, a sense of continuity. A chance to grow up in one place. That's one of the things I like about living here. I know our neighbors, and they know us."

Mike had lived in his L.A. apartment for five years and hadn't known even one of his neighbors. Of course, he was gone a lot, but even if he'd come home every night, he still wouldn't have made friends with anyone. He preferred to be alone.

"This is a different world for me," he said.

"I'm sure it is. Minivans, schools, churches on every corner."

Damn. He'd forgotten. "Cindy, some lady came by while you were out and left you something." Using the table for leverage, he pushed to his feet, then limped toward the foyer. The sheet of paper was where he'd left it on the hall tree. He limped back and handed it to her.

She scanned the flier. "I'm glad she stopped by. I'd nearly forgotten." She grinned at him. "I guess you don't have any blood to spare."

"Not this week. Ah, Cindy, I didn't think when she rang the doorbell."

Her eyes widened. "Oh, Lord, you didn't pull a gun on her, did you? Was she about five feet tall, kind of round with gray curls and wearing a hat?"

"That's her and no, I didn't threaten her with a gun."

"Thank goodness. Miss Vanmeter is one of the most conservative members of the church. She's a spinster and not very forgiving of us 'young people,' as she calls anyone under forty."

He swallowed and leaned against the island for balance. "I'd just gotten out of the shower. I was shaving. I came to the door in my towel. I didn't mean to flash the church lady."

Cindy covered her mouth with her hand, but he could tell she was giggling. "The woman won't go to a movie that isn't rated G. I'm sure she'd never seen a naked man in her life."

"I wasn't naked. I was wearing a towel."

"It was probably the highlight of her year."

"She thinks we're living together."

That sobered her up. "Oh, my. Okay. I'll call the church secretary and explain." She drew in a breath. "I've never been involved in a scandal before."

"There's more."

"The towel fell off? She made a pass at you?"

"I met Beth. She was standing in her yard while Miss Vanmeter was avoiding eye contact. We waved and said hello. Actually, she's the one I thought about flashing."

"Oh, I hope you didn't. She would have enjoyed it too much."

"That's what I thought."

Light color stained her cheeks. Little lines crinkled by her eyes. He was close enough that he could inhale the faint scent of her perfume. He liked the fragrance, and the way her laughter made him want to smile. He lived in a world of shadows, dodging death and trying to outwit assassins. Cindy lived in a world of normalcy and light.

Without thinking, he reached out and touched the tip of her nose. "I'm sorry for making trouble with Miss Vanmeter."

Electricity arced up his arm, through his chest and settled low in his belly. He couldn't pull away fast enough. Cindy's humor faded and she caught her breath as if she, too, had been burned.

He backed up and took his seat at the table. She continued to put away groceries. They talked, but the connection had been broken, severed by a physical awareness he couldn't shake.

"I should probably be leaving," he said. Usually, he couldn't wait to get away, but this time, even though he mouthed the words, he didn't want to move out of Cindy's house. Which meant it was past time to go.

"You can't even carry two bags of groceries in from the car," she said, opening the refrigerator and putting away margarine. "Wait until Monday. That's another four days away. If you try to do too much before you're ready, you'll just end up sick again."

She had a point. "Okay, I'll leave Monday."

She tossed him another empty bag, then leaned against the counter and folded her arms over her chest. "The kids are going to miss you."

"Why?"

"You play games with them, watch those horrible cartoons and tell them great stories. Why wouldn't they miss you?"

He wasn't sure that anyone had ever missed him before. "They've been coming in my room," he said. "I wasn't trying to—"

She held up her hands, palms out. "You don't understand. The fact that they're going to miss you is a good thing. It means they like you."

"Oh. I like them, too." He frowned. He liked children? When had that happened?

"Don't look so concerned. I'm sure it will wear off. Soon we'll all be a distant memory."

"How long has Allison had Shelby?"

"Since about six months after Nelson and I separated." Cindy carried the cartons of detergent into the laundry room, then closed the door. "It was about the time I told her that her daddy and I were getting divorced." She bent down and reached into one of the cupboards. After pulling out a tall machine, she set it on the counter, then added tea leaves and water. She flipped the switch. "I've spoken to a counselor about it. I even took Allison in a couple of times. The woman told me it was pretty normal. When Allison is ready, she'll let her imaginary friend go. In the meantime, it gives her some security."

She pulled out the chair across from his. "I never had an imaginary friend, so it doesn't make sense to me."

"Allison is a good kid."

"You know this because you've had so much experience?"

"I know people."

She sighed. "I hope you're right. She's my baby girl. I just want her to be happy."

He wanted to comfort Cindy, but he didn't have any words. Nor did he want to risk touching her again. Lusting after her in the privacy of his own mind was one thing, touching her was quite another. Besides, she'd felt the spark, too, and the last thing either of them needed was the messy entanglement of a relationship.

The sound of the tea machine was loud in the silence. Cindy bit her lower lip. The ringing of the phone rescued them both.

She jumped up and grabbed the portable from its cradle mounted on the wall. "Hello?"

He watched as her concern faded and she smiled. "Grace! Are you really in Hong Kong? This is an amazing connection." She paused, then winked at Mike. "He's doing great. When I came home from the market, he was bench-pressing the sofa in the family room." She listened. "Uh-huh. No, it's going fine. He hasn't been any trouble. He's right here. Why don't you talk to him yourself?"

He took the phone. As usual, before he could say hello, Grace was off and running.

"Michael? Are you okay? I called last week, but Cindy said you were pretty out of it. If I'd known you were hurt that badly, I would have stayed home. When I visited you in the hospital, you made it sound like a scratch."

He eyed the outline of the bandage visible through his jeans. "It is a scratch. It just happens to go through to the other side."

"Eeewww, that's gross." He could picture Grace wrinkling her nose. His sister looked nothing like him. She was short and blond, with bright blue eyes. He didn't care that they had different fathers or that she was almost ten years younger than he. She was the closest thing to family that he had. Being around Cindy and her kids made him realize that was important.

"Are you being nice to Cindy?" Grace asked.

"Of course. I'm very polite." He glanced at the subject of their conversation. She was pulling out bread and luncheon meat for sandwiches.

"That's not what I mean and you know it. She's very sweet and she deserves better than being dumped by her husband. So look out for her. Also, don't hide out all the time. Go outside. Sit in the sun."

"It's nearly a hundred degrees here," he reminded her. "The humidity is almost as high."

"Stop whining. I'm just saying you shouldn't stay in the house alone all the time. My friends are going to be checking on you. Be nice."

The doorbell rang. Cindy left the kitchen.

"I'm going to want a full report when I get back," Grace said.

"From me or your friends?"

She laughed. "Both. By the way, what do you think of Cindy?"

The curiosity in her tone belied the casualness of the question.

"Grace," he growled.

"She's very pretty," she went on, ignoring him. "Smart, a great mother. I think you'll like her."

"She's amazingly virtuous," Mike agreed. "But I'm too old to be set up with one of your friends. I'm fine. Go back to your husband and run his life."

"Mi-ke!"

"Say goodbye, Grace."

"I'll call next week. I love you. Bye."

With that, the line went dead. He stared at the portable phone for several seconds before pushing the off button. She always said the same thing at the end of every conversation.

"I love you."

How easily she spoke the words. As if saying them was simple. As if the thought of love was something she could grasp.

He stood up and limped to the wall, then hung up the phone. He wondered if Cindy knew Grace was matchmaking. Not that it was going to make a difference. Cindy wasn't his type. Hell, he didn't have a type.

Cindy walked into the kitchen and handed him a business card. He glanced at the small pink card and frowned. "What's this?"

"Mary Ellen is our local representative for this line of cosmetics." She pointed to the gold-embossed name curling across the card. "Her company has just started a line of men's skin-care products, and she stopped by to offer you a free facial."

"Why?"

Cindy returned to the refrigerator and pulled out jars of mayonnaise and mustard. "You're a single, good-looking guy, and Mary Ellen is..." She looked at him. "Let's just say I wouldn't recommend turning my back on her if I were you."

He tossed the card on the table as if it had burned him. "This is a scary place."

"Sorry, Mike. You'd better get used to it. Face it, you're about the most exciting thing to happen around here since they filmed a toilet-paper commercial at the local grocery store. You've got a very romantic profession, you've been shot. All the maternal types want to baby you, the single women want to marry you, the unfaithful wives want to sleep with you. You're a hot commodity."

He almost asked what *she* wanted. But that would have been stupid. He was occasionally a jerk, but he rarely acted without thinking. "I feel like a minnow in a pool of piranhas."

"Not a bad analogy." She picked up two packages of luncheon meat. "Roast beef or turkey?"

"Beef."

"Don't worry," she told him. "Somehow I think you can take care of yourself."

"We're about to find out. I don't even know the rules here."

"They're simple. I'll explain them as I go. Rule number one—don't wear a towel when you answer the door."

"So it's better to be naked?"

She grinned. "It would certainly be memorable. Although you might want to wear clothes to the barbecue Saturday. After all, Beth is going to be there."

He shuddered. "I'm counting on you to protect me."

She tore off several pieces of lettuce and handed them to him. "Go wash these, please."

As he took them, their hands brushed. The electricity leaped between them again. Their gazes locked for a moment, then they both looked away. Cindy might be willing to protect him from Beth, but who was going to protect him from himself?

Cindy stood in the upstairs guest room and studied her outfit in the mirror. It was only eight-thirty on Saturday morning, but she was up, had showered and put on makeup and was now trying to decide what to wear. She hated herself for caring.

"It doesn't matter," she said out loud. "He's not even going to get out of the car."

It wasn't as if she wanted Nelson back. She wasn't trying to impress him. It was just a matter of pride. She glanced at the clock and swore. She'd wasted the better part of an hour trying to look her best, when Nelson was simply going to honk the horn. She was a fool. Worse, she was pathetic.

With that, Cindy stuck her tongue out at her reflection and left the room. She turned right and walked to the two bedrooms at the end of the hall. There was a bathroom between them. Both doors stood open.

"Are you guys about ready?" she asked.

Allison stepped out of her closet. "I'm packed, Mommy, but Shelby doesn't want to go. She likes Mike and wants to stay with him."

"It's important for you to see your father," Cindy said. "I'm sure Shelby would miss you if she stayed behind."

"Shelby will come with me," Allison said quickly, her green eyes widening. "She was just wondering if we could stay home this one time."

"Sorry." Cindy moved into the room and checked her daughter's suitcase. "You have a toothbrush in there?"

"I still have to brush my teeth."

"Then go do it."

Cindy moved through the bathroom, into the second bedroom. Allison's room was all ruffles and lace with stuffed animals filling the corners. Jonathan's room was spare by comparison. He kept most of his sports equipment in the garage. The built-in shelves in the closet kept his toys tidy. On his ninth birthday, Cindy had bought him a computer and several software programs. It sat on the desk in front of the window and that's where he spent a lot of his time.

"Are you packed?" she asked.

Jonathan didn't look up from the screen. "Uh-huh. I packed my toothbrush. You don't have to ask."

"Good." She bent down and kissed her son's head. "You have a good time with your dad. Be polite to him and to Hilari."

Jonathan put down the joystick and looked up at her. Brown eyes, Nelson's eyes, stared at her. "She's just a dumb old girl," he said.

She smiled. "I love you, too."

With that, she left the room. She hated alternate weekends. First there was the rush of getting the children ready, and then they were gone. She couldn't even spend her morning cleaning up the kitchen. Nelson took the kids out to breakfast, so she didn't have to prepare anything.

She walked down the stairs, turning at the landing in the middle and following the staircase that led to the kitchen. The stairs were in the shape of an upside-down Y, with one leg leading to the living room and the other going to the kitchen. The smell of coffee greeted her.

"I hope you don't mind," Mike said, motioning to the already full pot.

"I think it's wonderful." She poured herself a cup, then glanced at the plastic containers, bowls and frying pan. "Are you cooking?"

"Pancakes. It's about the only thing I can make well."

"Sounds great."

He'd been in the house nearly two weeks and mobile for about nine days, but she still wasn't used to coming downstairs and seeing him in the kitchen. For one thing, he was too good-looking. A man like him should be saved for special occasions. She was used to something slightly more ordinary in her everyday life.

Now that his bullet wound had almost healed, he'd replaced his jeans with shorts. While she admired the tanned expanse of muscled leg, she wished he would go back to the denim. It was easier to concentrate when he wasn't so exposed.

He motioned to the empty bowl. "I don't know how many to make."

"I can probably force myself to eat four small ones," she said.

"What about the kids?"

She put her coffee on the counter and shrugged. "They won't be eating with us. It's their weekend to go with their father."

"And you're leaving, too?"

"No, why?"

"You're sort of dressed up."

She stared at the shorts and shirt she'd put on. The silk outfit had been on sale, otherwise she wouldn't have bought it. She was wearing makeup and she usually didn't bother. Her hair was curled. No wonder Mike thought she was going somewhere.

"Ignore me," she said.

He moved close to her. "What's wrong?" he asked.

The overhead lights caught the various shades of brown in his hair. The colors ranged from dark blond to gold to chestnut. His military cut was growing out. In another couple of weeks he would pass for a civilian. His T-shirt emphasized his strength. She desperately wanted him to hold her. Just for a minute, until the feelings of inadequacy went away. A foolish wish. Mike was just passing through. It wasn't his fault that every time he touched her, her knees turned to marshmallows.

There was a clatter on the stairs. Both kids came running down, banging their small overnight suitcases against the railings.

"Careful," she called.

They skittered to a stop when they saw the open containers. "Whatcha cooking?" Jonathan asked.

"Pancakes," Mike answered, limping back to the island and picking up the flour. "Your mom said you'd be having breakfast with your dad."

"But I want Mike's pancakes," Allison wailed.

"Hey, I'll make them next week," he said.

"Promise?"

He bent over and tugged on her blond braid. "Cross my heart."

"You guys aren't going to do anything fun while we're gone, are you?" Jonathan asked.

"We'll be as boring as we are old," Cindy said. "Besides, we're going to Mrs. Davis's for a barbecue tonight. If you guys stayed, you would have to come."

She heard the sound of a car engine and looked out the kitchen window. A sleek red convertible pulled up in front of the house. Nelson honked the horn, then stepped out of the car. The children grabbed their suitcases and raced toward the door. Cindy followed more slowly.

At the front door there were frantic kisses and calls of goodbye. Nelson waited by the now-open trunk and waved to his children, but he didn't glance at Cindy. She knew they would be back tomorrow promptly at four-thirty. If there had been a change of plans, Nelson would have had his secretary call and tell her.

Without wanting to, she peered at the front passenger seat. She couldn't see much of Hilari except for her long, dark curls. Cindy had seen the woman close up once. She was startlingly beautiful with long legs and a perfectly flat stomach. She was also very young. Maybe twenty-two. Nelson was nearly forty.

As the kids climbed into the car, they stopped to hug Hilari. Cindy felt a stab of pain in her heart. She knew her children loved her, but watching them with bimbo number two was difficult.

She waved until the car turned on the cul-de-sac then sped off. She closed the door and slowly walked back to the kitchen.

"I hate her," Cindy said as she grabbed her coffee and sat down at the table. "I suppose it's transference. I don't want to hate Nelson because I might say something to the children, and I don't want to make it harder on them. So I hate her." She took a sip of the hot liquid and grimaced. "I wish he would pick them up Friday night so I could get drunk or something, but what is there to do at nine on a Saturday morning?" She shook her head. "I sound pretty pathetic. Did you see her?"

Mike was measuring milk. "Who?"

"Nelson's girlfriend. Hilari. One *L*, and an *I* instead of a *Y*."

"You're kidding? Yeah, I saw her. So?"

"She's very beautiful. Even younger than the woman he left me for. Nelson kept his trophy wife for nearly a year, but they've separated now."

He cracked an egg, then looked at her. "Let me get this straight. You're upset because your ex-husband is dating some skinny teenager who can't even spell her name? Cindy, you're a beautiful woman, you've got great kids. Nelson is obviously a fool as well as a cad. Forget him." He picked up a fork and began stirring the batter.

She stared at him. His words floated around in her brain, then sort of settled in place. Mike thought she was beautiful. He'd said it casually, as if it was an obvious fact. The way most people would comment on the color of her eyes, or her hair.

She sipped her coffee and grinned. The most gorgeous man she'd ever met was standing in her kitchen, cooking her breakfast, telling her that her ex-husband was a jerk and that she was beautiful. If Mike kept that up much longer, she wouldn't have any choice—she would have to fall for him.

Chapter Five

"I thought it would look like Tara from *Gone With the Wind*," Mike said as they pulled up to the country club.

Cindy glanced at the large white building in front of them. It sprawled out on either side. To the left was the swimming pool where the kids' swim team practiced and had meets, beyond that, the tennis courts. On three sides was the private golf course. She suspected living close to the golf course was one of the few things Nelson missed about their marriage.

"Southern Gothic would have been too obvious," she said. "They went for a sort of art deco look, instead. More contemporary." She left the keys in the ignition and took the parking stub the valet handed her.

Mike had already opened the side door on the passenger's side. She grabbed her small gym bag. "It's pretty crowded on weekends," she said, pointing to the cars filling the parking lot. "When you come on your own, you don't have to use the valet. I thought it would be easier today."

Mike picked up his bag and slid the door of the minivan closed. "I appreciate it. I wouldn't want to use up all my strength walking to the gym only to collapse once I got there. I appreciate your bringing me."

"It's no trouble. We'll get you signed up. Grace has a family membership, so you can easily be added for the summer. In addition to the gym, there's tennis and golf. Oh, the restaurant's pretty good, too."

He held open the front door for her. As she walked past him, she noticed her eyes were level with his throat, just as they had been with Nelson. But somehow, Mike seemed larger than her ex-husband.

"I've never understood the purpose of golf," Mike said, following her to the reception desk. "It seems like a perfectly good way to ruin a walk."

She laughed. "You need to say that quietly around here. People take their golf very seriously. There are seven courses within a fifteen-minute drive."

When they reached the reception desk, the young woman there smiled at both of them. Her gaze drifted over Cindy, then settled on Mike. Cindy almost heard her intake of air. "Good morning," she said, her voice nearly a purr. "How may I help you?"

Cindy leaned on the countertop. "My friend, Mr. Blackburne, is staying at his sister's house for the summer while she's away. He would like to use the facilities here. His sister has a family membership. I have the card right here."

She held it out. The woman, barely out of her teens, couldn't seem to tear her gaze away from Mike. Cindy waved it in front of the receptionist's face. "Miss? The card?"

"Oh." The woman blinked. Her smile broadened. "It will be no trouble, Mr. Blackburne. Would you like a tour of the facilities? I would be happy to take you myself."

Mike shook his head. "Cindy's going to take me around."

The younger woman flashed Cindy a look of pure hatred. Cindy couldn't help it. She slid close to Mike and looked up at him. "It's simply no trouble," she said, staring into his brown eyes.

Suddenly, what started out as a childish bid to claim a relationship that didn't exist quickly turned into something else. As he met her gaze, she realized his eyes weren't brown at all. They were all colors. Flecks of gold and hazel and brown and tiny dots of blue. His pupils dilated and her knees weakened. Without wanting to, she placed her hand on his forearm. The tingling began in her fingertips and worked its way up to her shoulder, across her back and down her chest. It was difficult to breathe, and she could have sworn she heard music.

He'd shaved that morning and his jaw was smooth. Her fingers itched to touch his skin, to feel the heat there. His mouth was firm. What would it feel like against—

Cindy jerked her hand away and bit back a yelp. What on earth was she thinking about? This was insane. She glanced at Mike out of the corner of her eye, but he was signing a form the receptionist had given him. It was as if the incident had never happened. At least not to him.

A few moments later, she was still fighting the effects. The skin that had touched his was both hot and cold. Her breathing was rapid, her breasts achy. Hormones, she told herself firmly. It was just a weird time in her monthly cycle. Or maybe Beth was right and she'd been living too innocently for too long. Maybe she should think about dating, or therapy. Whatever the solution to her problem, it sure wasn't Mike Blackburne.

"If you need anything, Mr. Blackburne, I mean anything at all, please let me know." The receptionist picked up a card and wrote something on it, then handed it to him. "Enjoy your stay."

"Thanks," Mike said.

They turned away from the desk. Cindy headed them toward the stairs. "The locker rooms are down here," she said. "Along with the weight room and the aerobics classes. You probably don't want to take a step class anytime soon."

He shook his head. "I've got to build up the muscles slowly. They've been ripped pretty bad."

She shuddered. "Maybe you need a new line of work. What you do sounds scary."

"Not as scary as this." When they reached the bottom of the stairs, he handed her the business card the receptionist had handed him.

She scanned the printed words. They named the country club, stated the hours it was open and gave a number to call. "So?"

"Turn it over."

She did. On the back, someone had written: *I'm Heather. Call me anytime. For anything.* The last word was underlined three times and followed by a phone number. Cindy felt her eyes widen. "My goodness, she was hitting on you."

"Yeah." He tugged at the collar of his T-shirt.

He looked so genuinely surprised and uncomfortable, she laughed. "Oh, Mike, she's just a kid. Maybe twenty. I'm sure a big, bad bodyguard like you could handle her."

"I'm not so sure. Kids are maturing earlier these days. She could probably teach me a few things."

The hallways downstairs were more narrow than the spacious upper rooms. As they were talking, several people passed. All the women eyed Mike, then said hello. At first, Cindy thought she was imagining it, but by the time the third woman paused to smile and greet, she knew it was real.

"You're very popular," she said.

Mike swallowed. "Why?"

"I'm not sure. You can't be the only good-looking guy in the building."

"Gee, thanks."

She glanced up at him, then covered her mouth. "Sorry. You know what I mean."

"Uh-huh. Sure. Why don't you show me where the locker rooms are."

She walked to the end of the corridor and turned the corner. There was a large door marked Men, and across from that was the ladies' locker room.

"Are you going to work out?" he asked.

She hesitated. She walked regularly, although it was difficult in the summer because of the heat. She'd been fighting five pounds for about two months and currently the extra pounds were winning. "I thought I might use the treadmill," she said.

"Great. Let's meet here in five minutes."

Before she could answer, the door to the ladies' locker room opened and a stunning brunette stepped into the hallway. She was closer to forty than thirty, but had the face and figure of a beauty queen ... or that actress who had played Wonder Woman on television. Cindy sagged against the wall. Timing. It was all about timing. Two minutes later and they would have missed her. But no. Here she was—in the flesh.

Dark blue eyes met hers. The woman smiled. "Cindy. How good to see you. At the grocery store yesterday, I remember thinking you hadn't been to the club in a while. I'm so glad you're back." She patted her own flat stomach. "We can't let gravity win."

The so-called niceties taken care of, she swung her head toward Mike. The smile that had been merely pleasant became predatory. Her teeth were white enough to read by, Cindy thought grimly, still smarting from the dig about her weight.

"You must be Mike," the woman said, her voice low and sultry. "I'm Mary Ellen. Did you get my card?"

Mike looked blank for a moment, then he nodded. "Cindy gave it to me. It's really nice of you, but I'm not interested in—"

She raised her hand to cut him off. "I know. A man like you doesn't need any help. You're handsome enough on your own. But have you considered the fact that you'll be forty in another five or six years? Skin can be very unforgiving." She stepped closer and reached her fingers up to touch his cheek. "I'd hate to see all these good looks hidden behind some nasty wrinkles."

Cindy resisted the urge to stick her finger in her mouth and make gagging noises.

"Not today," Mike said and reached behind him. He got hold of the doorknob and turned it, then disappeared into the men's locker room.

"He's quite something," Mary Ellen said.

Cindy smiled tightly, then did a disappearing act of her own. As she peeled off her shorts and T-shirt and shimmied into a green Lycra leotard, she decided that bringing Mike to the club had been a bad idea. She should have just dropped him off at the curb and returned later to pick him up. There were too many women around. She felt like the kid who got a pony for her birthday and it arrived during the party; everyone got to ride it but her.

She shoved her clothes into a locker, then walked over to the mirror. Several women were on either side of her. She saw them looking at her, but none of them said anything. Thank goodness. A few hours ago, Mike had made her feel special when he'd told her she was beautiful and Nelson was a fool. Now she just felt dowdy and unnecessary. Like a shriveled-up appendix. Not that she wanted his attention. She didn't. It was just—

She sighed. She didn't know what it was anymore. Nothing made sense. She slipped a headband over her head, then pulled her hair back into a ponytail. It wasn't very long, so the ends only stuck out a couple of inches. She adjusted the headband so her bangs were off her face, then frowned at the reflection in the mirror. She was still wearing her makeup. She was going to sweat it off in about fifteen minutes.

"An attractive look for summer," she muttered as she left the locker room. "Raccoon eyes and streaked cheeks."

Mike was waiting in the hallway, speaking to a blonde. As soon as he saw her, he pushed off the wall and moved close.

"Get me out of here," he whispered into her ear.

"The gym is this way."

They entered the mirrored room. About half the equipment was in use. "I'll be over there," Cindy said, pointing to the row of treadmills at one end.

Mike nodded. "I'm going to use the weights. It'll take about forty-five minutes."

Great. He could lift weights longer than she could walk on the treadmill. And he hadn't even seemed to notice the way her sleeveless leotard clung to her body. Of course, judging by Mary Ellen's cracks about her weight, he probably didn't want to. *I need this day to start over,* Cindy told herself.

"Why don't we meet out in front in an hour?" she said. "Perfect."

He turned toward the machines. She waited, hoping he would wave, or watch her walk to the treadmill, but he seemed absorbed in the equipment. She gave a sigh of defeat and moved down the center aisle. She wondered if she looked like Allison did when she pouted.

Mike glanced around the gym and wished it weren't so new. He was used to seedy places with concrete-block walls and dirty windows. Here the lighting was concealed, the mirrors sparkling clean and the carpeting nicer than anything he'd had in his apartment.

He was also dressed all wrong. He saw that right away. His tattered shorts and cutoff T-shirt made him stand out even more. The women were wearing matching outfits that clung to every curve. On some of them, like Cindy, it looked great, but a few of the women looked as if they'd been starving themselves.

He walked over to the leg press and adjusted the weight down. His right leg was strong, but his left would have to be built up slowly. It would have been easier if it had been his arm. Then he could have used free weights.

He settled in the seat and began to press. Instantly, pain shot from his thigh to his ankle, then up to his groin. He breathed slowly and worked through the discomfort. After a few repetitions, it faded to a manageable ache. Slowly and steadily, he told himself. It was going to take three months to build up his strength again.

He ignored everyone around him. It was safer. In the two minutes he'd spent waiting for Cindy, three women had approached him, offering everything from a home-cooked meal to a massage. More unsettling than their invitations was the fact that they all knew who he was. It made him nervous. He was used to being in the background. In his line of work, he blended with the other men in suits. When someone looked at him, they didn't know if he was an assistant, a superior or the bodyguard, and that's how he liked it.

He stood up and adjusted the weight a little higher, then repeated the exercise. This time he glanced around. He found if he turned his head just so, he could watch Cindy in one of the mirrors without looking anywhere near her. Of course, he could only see her from the rear, but it was still a great view.

She had a perfect butt. Not flat, but round. He imagined holding it, squeezing it, nibbling it. Her hips flared out from her waist. She was curvy. He didn't understand women who wanted to look like teenage girls. Women were supposed to be soft and yielding. The bumps and dips were the best part. Of course, who was he to judge?

He finished his reps, then stepped over to another machine. The door opened and two men came in. One had a beerbelly and both had thinning hair. From the way they ogled the women exercising, Mike figured they were here just for the view. He ignored them and set the weight on the leg-curl machine. He could feel the sweat popping out on his back. It hurt like a sonofabitch, but he kept going.

One of the men—the one wearing a T-shirt advertising a local dance club—walked to the leg-press machine. He glanced at the weight and did a double take. "Someone let their kid in here?" he asked no one in particular.

Mike ignored the comment and continued working. He massaged the muscle between reps and reminded himself it couldn't be healed in a day.

He walked over to the next piece of equipment. Beerbelly followed. He glanced at the weight, then Mike. His thick eyebrows drew together, then he made a big show of moving the weight higher. Much higher.

They repeated the procedure twice more. Mike was starting to feel as if he was in a contest. Everyone was watching him. He wanted to tell the guy he'd been shot in the leg and fell off a building and that's why he was working light weights. He wanted to tell himself it didn't matter. But his ego wasn't listening. Occasionally, he glanced at Cindy. When she saw him, she waggled her fingers at him. Her breasts moved with each step. That was enough to distract him from his bad temper.

It had been a mistake to come here on a weekend. He would skip tomorrow, not only because it would be crowded, but because the muscle would need to rest, then he would limit his workouts to the middle of the week. He didn't need the aggravation.

Cindy stepped off the treadmill and grabbed a towel to wipe her face. He glanced at his watch, then limped over to her. "Are you done?" he asked.

"Yeah. Twenty-five minutes is all I can do today." She was flushed and sweating.

"I'm about done, too," he said.

"I thought you said it would take you forty-five minutes."

He glanced at the crowded room. Most people looked away when he caught them watching him, although a few of the women continued to stare boldly. Beerbelly was adjusting the weights up, yet again, on a machine Mike had used.

"I'm tired out," he said. "And I don't dare take a shower here. They'll probably sell tickets."

"I'm sorry."

"It's not your fault."

He glanced at the bench press, then at her. "I'll meet you in the hall in a couple of minutes. I have to do one more machine."

After she left, he went over to the bench press. He adjusted the weight, then got in position. He focused all his attention on raising the bar. His muscles protested, but he did twenty slow reps. Then he grabbed a towel and started for the door.

Once there, he paused. Beerbelly had followed him to the machine. He looked at the weight, then at Mike. His eyes widened with disbelief. Beerbelly settled on the bench and tried to lift the bar. It didn't budge. Mike gave him a mocking salute, then left the room.

When he was settled in the passenger seat of the minivan, he acknowledged to himself that he'd behaved like a child. Damn, it had felt good, too.

"You okay?" Cindy asked.

"Yeah. Just a little overwhelmed. I know you mentioned there weren't a lot of single guys in the neighborhood, but I was afraid for my life in there."

"I think it's your career." She stopped at the bottom of the slight hill and made a right by the fountain. "It's very romantic, if you don't mind your significant other risking his life. Face it, Mike. You're a hot prospect."

He didn't want to ask for what. "Why don't you date, Cindy?"

"How do you know I don't?"

"I heard you talking with Beth."

"Oh. I forgot." She cleared her throat. "Yes, well, it's difficult for a woman with children. A lot of men aren't interested, for one thing. For another, dating requires a certain amount of time and energy. I don't want to miss my kids' best years because I'm trying to have a social life.

It's hard to balance what I want and my needs with what's best for them. Right now, I'm giving them more and myself less. I think in time that will change."

"I admire your dedication," he said. "Your kids are lucky to have you."

They'd turned onto the main street, but instead of studying the familiar road, he pictured his own empty childhood. How would things have been different if his mother had been a little less concerned about herself and a little more concerned about him?

"I'll ask you to repeat your praise the next time they're furious at me for something," she said.

"Be my guest."

He glanced at her. She was smiling. He could see her dimple and the curve of her cheek. She'd thrown a T-shirt over her green leotard. Her long legs were bare. He wanted to run his fingers along her thighs and feel her silky skin.

It was the wrong thing to think about, so he focused on her hands, the smooth short nails, the delicate wrists. Why had Nelson left her? Cindy had said something about a trophy wife, but why would any man want someone other than her? She was funny, bright, incredibly sexy and a great mother.

"What are you thinking?" she asked.

He slid his gaze away and stared out the front window. "I was wondering about lunch."

"We have to eat light. The barbecue is tonight, and the food is always amazing."

He'd forgotten about that.

"Get that panicked look off your face," she told him. "These people are my friends. You'll be safe."

He wondered what it would be like to have friends. He knew people, but he didn't spend time with many. What would it be like to live in one place, to come home to one woman? What would it be like to belong? He couldn't imagine. He'd never belonged anywhere in his life.

Cindy handed Mike a covered cake plate, picked up a bowl of potato salad from the hall table, then closed the front door behind them.

"Aren't you going to lock it?" he asked.

"We're just going across the street," she told him.

"You should at least make someone work if he's going to break into your home."

"If you insist." Shifting the salad bowl to her left hand, she opened the door, pulled the key out of the lock, closed the door, turned the key until the bolt shot home then looked at him. "Happy?"

"Very."

Cindy chuckled. "This is Sugar Land, Mike. Nothing bad happens here. I swear."

"You never know." He checked the cul-de-sac before stepping out onto the street. "I'm glad we're walking and not driving tonight. This cake looks lethal."

She glanced at the container he was holding. "It's called Black Russian Cake and it's wonderful. Be sure to take a piece. I got the recipe out of a romance novel I read last year. I think the author lives somewhere in town, but I'm not sure."

Despite the fact that it was after six, the air was still steamy. They hadn't had rain in a couple of days so the humidity had fallen below ninety percent, but the sun beat down unmercifully.

"I'm glad Beth has trees in her yard," she said. "It's going to be hot."

Mike grunted.

She looked at him. "What's wrong?"

"Nothing." But he was staring at the house in front of him as if he'd never seen it before.

She could hear voices from other couples already in the backyard. If she didn't know better, she would swear Mike was nervous. "Everything is going to be fine," she said.

He didn't answer. Before Cindy could question him more, Beth spotted them and came to the gate.

"You're here. I'm so pleased." With one smooth movement, she reached for the cake plate and held out her other hand. "You must be Mike. I'm Beth."

Mike shook hands with her. He smiled tightly as she chattered, then shot Cindy a look. She knew he was wondering if she'd told Beth that he'd overheard their conversation last week. She hadn't. She figured if she did, Beth would never dare show her face again.

Before she could intervene, Darren came forward and urged Mike into the backyard. The men had congregated around the two grills. There were six men, counting Mike. He was handed a beer and introduced.

Cindy thought about rescuing Mike but figured he'd been in more dangerous situations than this. After all, she knew these men and they were basically nice guys. She followed Beth into the kitchen.

The other four women were already there. They poured Cindy a glass of wine and instantly bombarded her with questions.

"So what's he really like?" Sally asked.

"He's a serious hunk," Christina said.

"What do the kids think of him?" Mary asked.

"Wait, wait." Beth held up her hands. "I want to go first. I have two questions. One, have you seen him naked yet? And two, how hard are you resisting temptation?"

Cindy set her container of potato salad on the counter and took the wine Sally offered. She settled on the stool by the bar. "I have nothing to say on the subject."

The other five women groaned in unison.

"You have to tell us something," Karen said, leaning close and poking her in the ribs. "I mean, we're all boring married ladies. You're the only one who gets to have any fun."

"Being divorced is a real blast," Cindy said. She felt her good mood slipping away.

Beth caught her eye and gave her a sympathetic smile. She quickly put the women to work, rolling paper napkins around plastic utensils. Soon Cindy's houseguest was forgotten amid the usual chatter and gossip.

She sipped her wine slowly. She knew these women. She carpooled with them, had been to their houses and had entertained them at her own. But in those few minutes of questions, she realized she was different. She was single and they were married. Funny, she'd never put that together before.

After the divorce, they'd all stood by her. It wasn't unusual not to have a husband at a social function. Most of the men in their circle traveled quite a bit, sometimes for months at a time. But she wasn't one of them anymore and it was unlikely she ever would be again.

She reached for a package of paper plates and began counting them. Beth came over and leaned against the counter. "Sorry about that," she said. "I didn't know they'd all jump on you."

"It's okay. They're curious." She glanced at her friend and smiled. "*You're* curious."

Beth lowered her voice. "Have you seen him naked?"

"Not yet, but when I do, you'll be the first to know."

"Gee, thanks."

Beth gave her a quick hug, then walked over to the oven. The ribs were being baked first so they would cook quicker on the grill. While the women were talking, Cindy slipped out the back door. She glanced at the men but didn't see Mike. She walked to the edge of the fence and stared at the sky.

The sun hadn't set yet and wouldn't for another hour or two. Heat rose from the sidewalk. Candles in glass jars had been placed around to ward off bugs, although she and Mike had sprayed themselves with insect repellent before leaving her house. She dropped her gaze to the pecan trees, then lower to children playing in the greenbelt.

She hadn't felt this alone since she'd been a teenager.

What had gone wrong? Why hadn't her marriage worked out? She grimaced. She knew the answer to the last question. Nelson was a jerk. Unfortunately, it had taken ten years and his walking out on her for her to see it. But that didn't explain how everything got so messed up. She'd had her whole life planned.

"You look serious about something," Mike said, coming up to stand next to her.

She shrugged. "What were you doing? Casing the joint? Checking out the perimeter?"

She'd been teasing, but Mike looked sheepish. "Some habits are hard to break."

"It's been several years since the last terrorist attack, soldier," she said. "Maybe you could not be on alert tonight."

"Maybe." He took a sip from his bottle of beer. "What's your excuse?"

"I miss my kids."

"What else?"

"I thought I'd be married forever." He offered her his bottle and she took a swallow. As a rule, she didn't like beer, but tonight the biting yeasty flavor tasted right. "I suppose that's what I get for trying to plan out everything. I was tempting fate."

He leaned against the fence, bumping her elbow with his. She could smell the faint scent of his skin. He was warm and tempting. She found herself wondering how she could get their bare legs to brush together without making a complete fool of herself. She couldn't come up with a plan and figured she would have to settle for looking at his legs. Bless the summer heat, she thought with a smile.

"There are always variables," he said. "You've got to learn to go with them. No matter how well I plan a job, there's always something. Some kid steps out in front of the car, the electricity goes off. When you least expect it, life throws you a curve."

"The ribs are ready," Beth said, coming out the back door and carrying a large tray. The men parted to let her through to the grill, then Darren took the tray from her.

"Mike, why don't you take the first watch?" Darren said, holding out the tongs.

Mike started toward the other man. When he reached the grill, he looked back at her and winked. Low in her belly she felt a flutter of awareness, of need and something slightly more dangerous. A tugging that went all the way to her heart.

It wasn't just that Mike was gorgeous, had a smile that could melt aluminum and a body worth worshiping. It was that he was also a nice guy. She had a feeling, a very bad feeling, that life had just thrown her a curve.

Chapter Six

It didn't take Mike long to figure out he didn't like barbecues. Grown men standing around an outdoor grill on a hot, muggy summer evening burning meat and fighting off bugs wasn't for him. If they wanted to go camping, *that* he could understand. He liked being away from civilization, pitting his skills against the wilds of nature. But this suburban ritual made no sense to him. The grills were gas, for God's sake, and the meat had already been partially cooked in an oven.

He took another swig of beer, then shrugged. Everyone else was having a good time. He didn't have to understand what they saw in it. In his business, he was used to watching other people do odd things. What made him nervous this time was that everyone knew who he was.

He liked his life in the shadows. When he guarded a political figure or a celebrity, all eyes were on the client. But here, in Beth's backyard, they knew his name, what he did for a living and the fact that he'd served in the military.

"I wish our football team had a chance at a winning season this year," Sam said. "It's Jeff's last year."

"He's going to play?" Darren asked.

"Running back. First string. But he's not going to try to make the team in college. He wants to keep his grades up. You follow football much, Mike?" Sam asked.

"I don't have the time."

"Too bad." Sam grinned. "Here it's nearly a religion. Especially the high school and college games." He turned his attention back to the grill.

Mike leaned against the fence and watched the men. They were all dressed the same, in shorts and T-shirts. They were around his age, at various stages of fitness and hair loss. He'd never thought of himself as middle-aged, but these guys looked it and they were his contemporaries. Maybe he needed a new line of work. He rubbed his thigh and thought that might not be a bad idea, but what else did he know how to do?

Darren turned the ribs over again. Mike's turn at the barbecue had been mercifully brief.

Jack, who was married to Christina—or was it Mary?—sat on one of the lawn chairs. "I've been thinking of getting one of those mowers you ride."

Darren laughed. "Your yard isn't any bigger than this one. Where you gonna ride it?"

"We're thinking of buying some property and building a cabin," Jack said.

Darren shook his head. "Then wait until you get the land. But if you need a chipper, I just got a great one. It would make mulch out of a chain-link fence." He poked at the ribs. "Beth wants to redecorate the living room."

All the men groaned. "Don't talk to me about decorating," Jack said. "I was thinking of doing something in a floral print." His voice was high. "How does this sample make you *feel?*"

Sam, tall and thin, with dark hair, motioned with his beer. "It took Sally three weeks to pick out tile for the guest bathroom. Three weeks!"

"And how much did it cost?" Darren asked.

"Don't remind me. For that price, it should have been installed by naked dancing girls."

Roger, a large man with a belly hanging over the waistband of his shorts, leaned forward and lowered his voice. "I have a new assistant. You should see this girl. Twenty-two, maybe. With big eyes and bigger—" He cupped his hands in front of his chest.

"You working overtime yet?" Jack asked.

Roger winked.

Mike took another swallow of his beer, draining the bottle. The sun had slipped low enough that the backyard was in shade. There was a long deck behind the house. Two tables had been set up, with paper tablecloths and plastic glasses. There were lawn chairs scattered on the grass. From the deck, a stone path led to an oval-shaped swimming pool with a large Jacuzzi at one end. He felt as if he'd traveled to a foreign country. The natives might speak the same language, but he didn't understand the subject matter. He also didn't want to hear about Roger's young assistant. It made him think about Cindy, and how Nelson had betrayed her.

He tilted his empty bottle. "I'm going to get another one," he said to no one in particular.

He limped into the kitchen. The women were gathered around the center island. It was a long counter with a sink in the middle.

Christina—or was it Mary?—was peeling a carrot. "He works so late, leaving me with the kids all the time, then he gets mad when they don't want to do things with him. Why would they? They're teenagers and have their own lives. He only has himself to blame. I've tried to explain that to him, but he won't listen."

"I worry about the same thing with Nelson," Cindy said. He didn't think she'd noticed he'd come into the kitchen. "He only sees them every other weekend. He can't have a relationship with them that way. I've told him I wouldn't mind if he saw them more, but he can't be bothered."

Sally shook her blond head. "Men. Do you know what I got for my birthday?"

There was a chorus of no's.

She looked up and grimaced. "A gift certificate for a year's worth of car washes."

Cindy laughed. Beth groaned.

"I know," Sally said. "It's pathetic. I told him I wanted a pair of gold hoop earrings. That's not too difficult. But it would have required him going to the mall on his own, and I'm sure he'd rather face a pack of rabid dogs."

"Darren will shop," Beth said. "I just wish he was more romantic. You know, flowers every now and then for no reason. Or maybe even call me up and say, 'Don't bother cooking, honey, let's go out.'" She straightened and shrugged. "He's a sweetie, really. If I ask him to go out, he always says yes, but sometimes I wish he would offer."

There was a murmur of assent.

Mike limped over to the refrigerator and pulled out a beer. Cindy saw him and walked over.

"How are you doing?" she asked quietly.

He moved toward the back door and she followed. "My leg aches, but otherwise I'm fine." He glanced at the group of women in the kitchen, then out at the men gathered around the grill. "Is it always like this?" he asked.

She followed his gaze. "The separation of the sexes? I suppose so. I hadn't thought about it. I think we all like spending time with our friends. These women see their husbands every day."

He supposed it made sense, but something felt off to him. The complaining, the being apart. "Do any of the people in these couples love each other?"

The question seemed to have surprised her. She tilted her head and smiled. "Of course, Mike. What would you think?"

That they didn't seem very happy to him. "I'm just observing the situation," he said. "Checking out the local customs."

"Check out the food," she said. "It's nearly time to eat."

She was right. The next few minutes were a bustle of activity, with salads and bread being set out on the tables and the men serving the meat.

Mike sat at the end of one of the picnic tables and used a stool to prop up his bad leg. He could feel the aching pain from the workout, not to mention the standing around he'd done earlier. He would pay for this activity tomorrow.

He was pleased when Cindy settled next to him. He didn't want to hear any more about Jack's lawn mower, or Roger's new assistant. But as Cindy asked him his preferences and scooped food onto his plate, he realized the dynamics of the group had changed. The men and women were no longer separate. They sat together, two by two.

Darren sat next to Beth. She was talking to Sally. Without glancing at her husband, she picked up a bottle of hot sauce and passed it to him. When he accepted the bottle, he bent forward and kissed her bare shoulder.

Roger sat on the end of a chaise longue with his wife's bare feet in his lap. In between bites, he massaged her toes and pressed her heels into his thigh. When she glanced at him, he murmured something Mike couldn't hear, and winked. His wife smiled and nodded.

They were all like that. Sitting together, exchanging private, unconscious touches, performing a ritual that somehow bonded them. They leaned against each other, brushed arms, kissed lightly, all the while talking with everyone around them.

He felt as if he'd come into a play during the second act and no one could explain the story. Deep in his chest, in a place he'd forgotten he had, he felt a twinge of regret. Perhaps at one time he could have learned the words and actions of this world, but it was too late now.

He looked over at Cindy. She was next to him, close, but they didn't touch. She didn't give him secret smiles or lean against him.

When the meal was over, the women cleared the table while the men sat around and discussed sports. Mike didn't have an opinion on the Houston Oilers. He'd never followed professional teams much. There wasn't any point in getting excited about a season when his work would force him to miss most of the games.

After a few minutes, Darren stood up and stretched. "All right, guys, are we all going to do it, or do you want to flip for it?"

Jack finished his beer. "We used paper plates. How much can there be? Let's just all do it."

With that, the men trooped into the kitchen and began cleaning. Mike followed along. He grabbed a dish towel and dried the serving bowls as they were passed to him. Darren collected trash, Roger washed, Sam put the leftovers in the refrigerator, Jack wiped off countertops.

The higher-pitched conversation of the women caught his attention. He peered outside. All six had changed into bathing suits and were sitting on the edge of the pool or slipping into the Jacuzzi. His gaze settled on Cindy. She'd put on a one-piece dark green suit that matched her eyes. A headband held her hair off her face, but his attention didn't stray much above her shoulders.

The suit hugged her curves, outlining her full breasts and emphasizing the shape of her hips. He felt his mouth grow dry. None of the other men seemed to notice their wives. He wondered how long he would have to be with Cindy before he ceased to appreciate her body and the way she moved. He supposed she wasn't anything extraordinary, but she appealed to him on a fundamental level. As if he'd been waiting for her all his life.

Nelson was a fool, he thought, not for the first time. Yet, he couldn't help being pleased by the fact that she was single. Of course, he wasn't going to do anything stupid like try to get involved. It would be crazy for both of them. They had nothing in common.

"I gotta check on the kids," Roger said, walking over to the wall phone by the refrigerator.

The heavyset man who'd implied an interest in his young female assistant spent fifteen minutes on the phone with his two children, who had been left without a sitter for the first time.

Jack and Darren joined their wives in the pool and swam around with them in their arms.

Mike stood in the kitchen and stared out the window, close to but not part of their world. What would it be like to have a family to come home to, to actually celebrate holidays instead of ignoring them? What would it feel like to commit to someone forever? To have children and a mortgage, maybe even a dog. How would his life be different if he had a place to come home to?

"You're limping more than you usually do," Cindy said, moving closer to Mike and fighting the urge to slip an arm around his waist. She doubted he would appreciate the help.

"I know." They closed the gate behind them and started down Beth's driveway. "I did too much at the gym."

"I'm sure standing around at the party didn't help." Even if he had looked mighty fine doing it.

Cindy smiled faintly, knowing he wouldn't be able to see her expression in the darkness. It was nearly eleven. They'd stayed late at the barbecue, swimming, and eating too much dessert. She patted her stomach and knew she would now be fighting six pounds instead of five.

She shifted the plastic bag containing the empty salad bowl and cake plate to her other hand. "Are you going to be able to make it?"

"Sure. As long as we go slow." He held on to the fence until they reached the house, then he started down the driveway. "You can go ahead if you'd like."

"No. I'd be afraid you wouldn't make it across the street. You can lean on me."

He shook his head. "I'm too heavy."

The streetlamp was two doors down and the circle of light didn't reach this far. They'd moved out of the range of Beth's back porch light. Night insects chirped and buzzed around them. It was still hot, but without the intensity of the sun. She could smell tropical flowers and cut grass.

Cindy had pulled a T-shirt over her swimsuit, but the rest of her clothes were in the plastic bag with the serving pieces. She swung the bag back and forth in time with their slow steps.

"Did you have a good time?" she asked.

"It was different."

"Hmm, why do I think that's a no?"

They'd reached the sidewalk. Mike paused. "It's not a no. I've never been to a barbecue before. It was unusual. I'm starting to learn your suburban rituals."

He drew in a deep breath. "If it's not too much trouble, could I put my arm around you?"

"Sure." She moved closer. "Lean as much as you need to. I'm stronger than I look."

His arm settled on her shoulders. She could feel his heat and inhale the scent of him. He smelled masculine. It had been a long time since she'd been this close to the opposite sex. Years, in fact, not counting brotherly hugs from her friends' husbands or the moments she had spent trapped under Mike on the sofa.

She placed her arm around his waist and held on. "You doing okay?"

"Fine. Sorry to be such a problem."

"It's no big deal. I should have noticed you were in pain." She tried not to notice how right it felt to be next to him. It was just because he was a good-looking man, she told herself. But she knew it was more than that, and it scared her to death.

"I'm glad we went tonight," she said, to distract herself. "Having plans on Saturday night helps me forget the kids are gone."

"You really miss them."

"Of course."

"But I heard you say you wanted Nelson to spend more time with them."

They inched their way down the driveway onto the street. She could feel Mike tense with each step. "It's hard for me when they're gone, but I believe children need a mother and a father. I'm doing the best I can, but I still want them to see Nelson. He doesn't want the responsibility, though." She sighed. "There's a father-daughter campout in a few weeks. He swears he's going to go with Allison, but I know him. About a week before they're supposed to go, he'll call and tell me that something's come up. That will break her heart. I think Nelson doesn't want to risk spending time alone with the children. I think he's afraid of them."

"This guy has a lot of problems, Cindy. You have great kids."

She felt a flush of pleasure. "You don't know any other kids, so why should I trust your judgment?"

"I just know." He limped silently for a minute then said, "If Nelson backs out of the campout, I'll go with Allison."

She stopped and stared at him. They were standing a little more than halfway across the street. The streetlight didn't reach here and there weren't any cars on the cul-de-sac.

"Why would you do that?"

"Why not? I like Allison, and I enjoy camping. It was one of the best things about being in the service."

"You're crazy," she told him. "We're talking about a father-daughter campout. There will be seventy or eighty little girls running around and getting into trouble."

"So?"

"You must have hit your head harder than you thought when you fell off that building."

Her tone was teasing. He glanced at her. "It's no big deal. I'm happy to go with her. Really. Why is that so hard to believe?"

Her eyes had adjusted to the darkness and she could make out his features. He was still good-looking enough to make her thighs overheat and her palms sweat. Right now they were standing so close, their hips brushed together. His arm was around her shoulders, hers was around his waist. If she was really foolish, she could pretend this was a romantic moment. That he was holding her because he wanted to and not because his leg was about to give out on him.

"You're very sweet," she said. Without thinking, she raised herself on tiptoe and leaned forward to kiss his cheek. "Thank you," she murmured just before she touched his skin.

But in that second, he turned his head and her lips brushed against his mouth.

Cindy froze. She told herself she should pull back, but the arm around her shoulders tightened. Besides, she didn't want to. She hadn't felt that shiver of anticipation in a long time, although she wasn't sure she remembered exactly how one kissed a stranger.

While she was still debating, Mike took the decision out of her hands. He bent his head closer and pressed his mouth to hers.

His lips were as firm as she'd imagined them to be. He didn't attack or invade; instead, he held the contact, prolonging it until the electricity crackled between them and she had to drop the plastic bag she was holding.

Her eyes were closed. It seemed like too much trouble to open them. He drew back slightly and murmured her name. She smiled at the sound of his voice. "You're so beautiful," he whispered. She knew she wasn't, but at that moment, she didn't care.

He pulled her firmly against him. She went willingly. His chest was broad and hard. Her breasts nestled against him as if they'd been as lonely as the rest of her. She angled her head so when he brought his mouth down on hers again, she could feel all of him.

He kissed with the slow thoroughness of a man who enjoyed the act for its own sake and not just because it was the quickest road to sex. He brushed her mouth back and forth, then touched her lower lip with his tongue.

She parted for him, wanting to taste him and feel him, but he didn't enter. Instead, he traced the shape of her mouth, learning every curve, as if later he might be called upon to describe it in detail. She raised her free hand to his shoulders and melted against him.

There was heat. From the concrete road, from the night air and from their bodies. The temperature between them rose until she felt the flames licking at her most feminine place.

He was rock-hard, the muscles in his back thick ropes that shifted and tightened under her fingers. The arms around her shoulders and waist tightened as if he feared she would want to escape. She thought of telling him that it had never crossed her mind, but she didn't want to interrupt his kiss.

He drew her lower lip into his mouth and suckled gently. He swept his tongue across her dampened skin, sending hot liquid need down her chest and into her breasts. She felt herself swelling, aching, reaching for him. Her hips pressed against his and she cradled the part of him that echoed her desire.

In the back of her mind, some small still-rational part of her compared him to Nelson. They were the same height so the pose should be familiar. But it wasn't. Mike bent toward her as if kissing her was the most important task of his day. Nelson had always made her stretch up to meet him. Their bodies were different. Nelson had been wider, softer. Mike was all hard planes and steely muscles. She hadn't kissed a man other than her ex-husband in nearly twelve years. She'd forgotten how wonderful kissing could be.

At last he entered her mouth. Instantly, all thought fled as she could only feel the gentle, smooth exploration. He tasted of the brandy they'd had, and deliciously of himself. She wanted to crawl closer, to be inside of him, feeling more. She wanted to touch him everywhere and be touched in return.

She stroked his back, his shoulders, then the short silky strands of his hair. His palms echoed her journey in reverse as he first buried his fingers in her hair, caressed her shoulders and back, then dipped lower to cup her derriere.

She arched her hips against him, bringing her belly into contact with his arousal. His body tensed and he groaned low in his throat.

"Cindy," he said softly, breaking the kiss and speaking into her ear.

She slid her hips back and forth, taunting them both. His breathing was harsh. He punished her with sharp nips on her earlobe, then soothed the spot with moist kisses. The shivers started there and rippled down to her knees.

As first kisses went, it was a pretty exciting one. She giggled.

"Is that a statement about my technique?" he asked.

"No, it's just..." She caught her breath as his hand slid up her hip to her waist. She opened her eyes and stared at him. "Mike?"

His face was taut with need, his mouth damp from their kisses. "What?" he asked.

"That was my first kiss since the divorce," she said quickly, suddenly too shy to look at him. "If I'd known it was going to be this good, I would have done it sooner."

He was silent so long she was forced to glance up at him. His eyes darkened with an emotion she couldn't read. "Mike, I'm sorry. I didn't mean anything by—"

He brought his mouth down on hers, effectively silencing her. She went to him willingly. His hand stayed on her waist, but she willed it to move higher. The ache in her breasts had reached a fever pitch she knew only his touch would soothe.

When he didn't react to her mental message, she tried something more direct. She swept her tongue into his mouth, touching him, tasting him. She rocked her hips against his, reaching her hands down to his rear and holding him in place. At last, his hand began to slide higher.

The sharp metal-against-metal squeak of a garage door being closed caught her attention. She broke the kiss and turned her head to listen. At that moment, she realized they were standing in the middle of the street where virtually anyone could see them.

"Oh, my," she murmured. "What will the neighbors think?"

Mike shifted away from her and straightened. He had to clear his throat before speaking. "That I'm the luckiest guy in town," he said. He cleared his throat again. "I'm going to stay out here for a little bit. Why don't you go on in?"

She wanted to protest. A part of her was willing to continue what they'd been doing—even let it build to its natural conclusion. But the sensible part of her brain screamed that was out of the question. She barely knew the man. They couldn't make love. Correction. There wasn't any love here. They couldn't have sex. She didn't do that with men she didn't know, and Mike, well, she didn't know Mike's thoughts on the subject, but she had a feeling she was the last woman he would choose.

She picked up the plastic bag she'd dropped and glanced at him. "Are you going to be all right?"

"Yeah. Just give me a minute to recover."

She liked that his voice was shaking a little. She walked the rest of the way across the road, stepped up onto the curb and headed for her front door. Her body was still humming from their encounter. But as she moved into the cool foyer and shut the door behind her, she realized how empty the house was, and how very alone she felt. Even when Mike came inside, he wasn't coming home to her.

Chapter Seven

He was in enemy territory without a survival guide, and he had no one else but himself to blame.

The grocery store was huge. Mike was used to small corner markets that carried one brand of only a few kinds of food, while sporting an impressive selection of beer and hard liquor. He limped in through the automatic door and entered a foyer. On one side was a machine that dispensed water, a full-size ice freezer, a popcorn machine that made the area smell like a movie theater and two large containers—one for paper bags, the other for plastic—with signs above them reminding shoppers to recycle.

There was another set of sliding doors, then he entered the store itself. And stopped in his tracks.

He had nothing to compare it to, but he knew he'd stepped into a strange and frightening land. There was merchandise everywhere. Not just food. From where he was standing he could see plants, a video-rental department, a pharmacy, a hot deli, a florist and a salad bar that would put most restaurants to shame.

He swore under his breath.

When he'd moved out of Cindy's that morning, she'd offered to go grocery shopping for him, so he wouldn't have to worry about stocking up on his first day alone. Foolishly, he'd turned her down. He hadn't wanted to be any more trouble. Besides, they'd spent the last forty-eight hours performing an elaborate dance of avoidance and lies. Not only had they tried not to be alone together—a real trick for most of Sunday while her children were gone—they'd both pretended to forget the kiss. Or maybe he'd been the only one pretending. Maybe she'd been able to dismiss it from her mind.

The memory of her soft mouth against his had kept him up all Saturday night. Two cold showers hadn't helped his painful condition, nor had trying to think about something else.

He'd kissed women before. He rarely went more than a few months without a bed partner, although the last year or so had been pretty lean. But it was more than need that made him relive every moment of her in his arms. It was something much more dangerous and he didn't want to know what it was.

Before his line of thought produced its usual and obvious reaction, he limped over to the grocery carts and pulled one loose. It slid out easily. No sticky wheels or wobbly carts out here, he thought as he headed for the produce section.

He needed everything. Grace had planned to be gone for at least three months, so both the refrigerator and pantry were empty. It hadn't taken him long to settle into his sister's place, probably because everything he owned fit into two duffel bags.

His way of life was strange to Cindy. He'd seen it in the look on her face when she'd helped him pack. She kept asking if he didn't have something else to take with him.

As he stared at the rows of perfect peaches and nectarines, he snagged a plastic bag from the roll at the end of the counter and remembered last night. It had been the best time he'd had in months. The kids had arrived home about four. He and Cindy had gone to the video store and rented a couple of movies. They'd ordered pizza, then made root-beer floats.

As he reached for a couple of nectarines, he tried to recall if he'd ever had a root-beer float before in his life. He'd sure never made one at home. The kids had laughed and Cindy had been smiling. Her green eyes had lit up with emotion as she stared at her children. She'd hugged them close, as if having them home was a precious gift, and they'd held on just as tightly. In that moment, he hadn't felt left out as much as envious. He wanted that for himself, too. A place to belong. Someone to belong—

His cart jerked in his hands. He turned his head and saw a petite dark-haired woman smiling at him.

"Oops," she said, and pulled her cart back. "Didn't mean to bump you." She glanced at the nectarines in his bag. "They're on sale this week."

"I hadn't noticed." He looked up at the sign. It was on a chalkboard and illustrated by a cartoonlike figure.

"The grapes are pretty cheap, too. And tasty." She reached into her cart and fumbled with a bag. When she straightened, she had a grape resting in the palm of her hand. "Try one."

"Ah, thanks." He took the grape, feeling vaguely like Snow White when she'd taken the apple in a movie he'd watched with Allison.

The tiny woman leaned toward him. "You're Mike Blackburne, right?" He must have looked confused because she laughed and placed her hand on his forearm. "I'm in a step aerobics class with your sister Grace. She told us all about you." Her eyebrows arched.

He started backing up. "Ah, it was nice to meet you..."

"Belinda," she said. "I was wondering if you might like to come over to dinner sometime."

He looked at her left hand and saw a diamond band sparkling there. "I'm not sure your husband would be pleased."

"Oh, he's gone a lot." Her smile broadened. "It could be our little secret."

"I'm not very good at keeping secrets," he said. "But thanks for asking."

With that, he turned his cart down the main aisle. He wanted to leave the store, but he needed food and it was unlikely the woman was going to pursue him in this public store.

"I'm in the book. Phone me if you change your mind," she called, then gave her last name.

He nodded and kept on going, slowing long enough to grab a bag of premade salad, and some broccoli. He cruised through the bakery department, searching for his favorite brand of bread. They must not make it in Texas, he decided after a few minutes of fruitless searching.

By the meat counter, two women shopping together tried to engage him in conversation, but he only smiled and kept on moving. He could feel a cold sweat breaking out on his back. It wasn't caused by exertion, he was barely moving at a fast walk. So it was something else. If he was honest with himself, he would admit he didn't like these people knowing who he was. It made him nervous.

He turned down the cereal aisle and picked out a box. At the far end were the paperback books and magazines. He paused there to find something to read. There was an entire section of the romance novels Cindy liked. He thought about picking one up for her, but didn't know which she might already have read.

He liked watching her read. She got lost in the story. Often he'd come into the family room and found her sprawled out on the sofa, one foot dangling over the back of the couch. How many times had he wanted to go to her? He'd known her skin would be soft before he touched it. He'd known she would taste of heaven long before they kissed.

Maybe that's what was bothering him. Usually, realities fell far short of the imaginings, but Cindy was even better than he'd hoped and he wasn't sure why. Of course he'd thought of kissing her, but the real thing had been different. Maybe because in the past kissing had been something he did on the road to going to bed with a woman. With Cindy, he'd enjoyed the act of kissing simply for itself. The process—holding her, feeling her lean against him, tasting her—had been enough. Although he didn't want to think about what could have happened if they'd been inside the house instead of standing in the middle of the street.

He picked up a book and flipped through it. But instead of words, he saw Cindy's face as it had been in the glow of the streetlight. He saw her swollen mouth and the passion in her eyes. Just thinking about it turned him on. But he knew it wasn't right. She was—

Another cart slammed into him. He looked up as a blond woman with an infant in the cart and a young girl trailing behind smiled at him.

"I'm sorry," she said. "I wasn't watching where I was going." She pointed at the book Mike was holding. "Does that look any good?"

"I don't know." He thrust the paperback at her, then grabbed his cart and hurried down the aisle. His injured leg screamed in protest, but he didn't slow down until he was safely lost in the canned goods.

Once there, he paused to catch his breath. They knew him. He could read it in their faces. They talked about him and when they got home they would call their friends and mention running into him in the grocery store. He'd heard they were interested, and it scared the hell out of him. He would feel safer in a roomful of armed terrorists. At least there he would know the rules.

Moving cautiously, making eye contact with no one and walking as quickly as his injury would allow, he walked to the aisle with soda and grabbed two twelve-packs. Up ahead were chips. He started toward them when a cart turned in at the far end. That sixth sense that told him to duck in time to avoid gunfire screamed for him to turn. He turned. As he whipped around to the center aisle, his peripheral vision registered a familiar form. Beth. He groaned. That was all he needed.

He was standing by the frozen foods. Mike quickly scanned the contents of the freezer, opened one glass door and pulled out five of the same dinner. He couldn't afford to be picky now. Before anyone else could speak to him, he made his way to the checkout counters.

Once there, he was trapped behind a prim woman who seemed to know everything about his wounds. For a moment, he was afraid she was going to ask to see the scar. Finally she left, helped to her car by an elderly box boy who was nearly twice her age and half her size.

Mike breathed a sigh of relief.

"How's it going?" the checker asked as she unhooked the front of his cart and started scanning groceries.

"You don't want to know," Mike said. He reached in his back pocket and pulled out his wallet.

"I haven't seen you in here before."

"I'm just visiting." He was mesmerized by how quickly she pulled his food across the small glass sensor. It beeped with the regularity of a pager going off.

"You're Mike Blackburne, right?"

His head snapped up and his attention narrowed. The woman was in her late twenties, with curly brown hair and blue eyes. "How did you know?"

She smiled. "Grace shops here all the time. We talk. She showed me your picture. If I'd known bodyguards were so handsome, I would have tried harder to get into trouble."

He swallowed. "It's not as romantic as it sounds."

"I don't know. It sounds pretty romantic to me." She glanced over her shoulder at the big wall clock above the produce section. "I get off work at three. Would you like to go for a cup of coffee?"

He fought the urge to whimper. "Thanks, but I've already got plans."

She took his money. "Too bad." After making change, she handed it to him. "I'm here Monday through Friday. Come by if you change your mind."

"I will. Thanks." He grabbed the two bags of groceries. Before he got outside, he was stopped twice more. The first time, a soft-spoken woman asked him if he would be willing to come to the Christian Women's luncheon to discuss security. He gave her Grace's phone number. The second woman didn't say much. She just looked at him as if he were a side of beef and she'd been starving for weeks. He literally jogged into the parking lot.

His leg was throbbing, he was dripping sweat and he hadn't even been to the gym yet. What the hell was going on here?

All he wanted was to escape. He reached into his shorts pocket and grabbed the keys. Then he scanned the row where he'd left Grace's white Ford Explorer.

"Dammit."

There were five white Ford Explorers sitting next to each other. They were identical. He hadn't thought to memorize Grace's license-plate number. Muttering under his breath, he hit the disarm button on the car alarm and walked past each one. The third vehicle beeped and snapped open the locks. He pulled open the door, shoved the groceries onto the front seat and scrambled up beside them. Barely stopping long enough to fasten his seat belt, he put the car in reverse and backed out of his space.

Once on the main road, he clung to the steering wheel as if it were a life belt and he were adrift at sea. He drove automatically until he reached his sister's subdivision. He pulled into her driveway and jumped out of the car. Without knowing what else to do, he crossed the lawn and went around to the back of Cindy's house. Her blue minivan was parked in front of the garage. He pounded on the back door.

When she pulled it open, she stared up at him. "Mike, what's wrong? You look awful."

He glanced over his shoulder. "They're coming," he said. "You've got to hide me."

For a moment, Cindy thought Mike had slipped into some delusional state. "Who's coming?"

He shook his head as if to clear it. A single lock of hair fell onto his forehead. "I went to the grocery store. They were everywhere. They kept talking to me and offering to squeeze my melons." He shuddered.

"Who?"

His dark eyes met hers. "Women."

She knew exactly what had happened. It wasn't hard to imagine, especially in a small community like this. Cindy took his hand and drew him into the house. "You're safe now. They won't hurt you here."

His breathing slowed to normal. He glanced down at her and frowned. "You're laughing at me."

She tried to keep the corners of her mouth from turning up, but she could feel herself starting to smile. "Maybe just a little. You were at the market, Mike. You make it sound like you just battled the thundering hordes."

"Yeah, well, you weren't there. They kept bumping into me with their carts. I don't understand how these women manage to drive around without getting into accidents, yet at the grocery store, they can't go two feet without bumping into something."

"Have you ever thought they were doing it on purpose?"

"Oh, God." He dropped his chin to his chest.

"Did you come right over when you got home?"

"Yeah. Why?"

"I was just wondering if you'd bothered to put your groceries away."

He swore. She giggled.

"You could try and be a little more sympathetic," he called over his shoulder as he marched out of her house.

Closing the door behind her, she followed him outside. "I think you're overreacting."

"So I shouldn't run in the opposite direction when I see Beth?" he asked as he fumbled with the passenger door. It was locked.

Before he ripped it off at the hinges, she plucked the keys dangling from his back pocket and hit the disarm button. Instantly all the doors unlocked. Mike jerked open the door and grabbed the two bags. She took one from him and started for Grace's back door.

"Running from Beth isn't necessary," she said as she set the bag on the counter and began to unpack the groceries. "I've told you. She talks a good game, but the truth is, she loves Darren. If she actually saw you naked, she would probably die from embarrassment."

"Let's not test your theory."

She pulled out a frozen dinner. The next one was the same. And the next. When she'd stacked all five together and placed them in the freezer, she glanced at him. "You really like Salisbury steak, don't you?"

He was shoving a bag of salad in the empty produce bin. He straightened and shrugged. "It seemed like a wise idea to get out of there as quickly as possible."

Sunlight streamed through the kitchen windows. Grace's house had a different floor plan from her own. This kitchen was long, with darker hardwood floors and brick accents. Mike leaned against the counter as if the morning's activities had worn him out.

His brown hair had grown out of its military cut. It was almost to his ears. He was still tanned and lean, his red T-shirt emphasizing the width of his shoulders and the muscles in his back. His shorts barely covered the bandage on his leg. He was tall, handsome and single.

"Like catnip to a cat," she said softly.

"What?"

"That's the problem. Look at where we are," she told him. "Nothing exciting ever happens here. Our business is families and raising children. We don't deal in international espionage."

He folded his arms over his chest. "How do you stand it?"

"How do you stand the city?" She emptied the second bag. After rinsing the fruit, she pulled a glass bowl out of Grace's cupboard and put the nectarines in it. Then she set the bowl in the refrigerator.

"The city is great," he said. "You can get anything, anytime you want. Movies, restaurants. Something is always happening. Not like here."

"I don't want anything to happen. Did you eat lunch?"

He shook his head.

"Come on. I'll make you a sandwich."

"Cindy, I moved out of your place this morning so I wouldn't be a bother."

"It's no trouble. I wasn't expecting you to leave so quickly. I've got plenty of food." She smiled. "You've had a harrowing experience. I don't think you should be alone just yet."

"Go ahead and mock me while I'm in a weakened condition." He followed her back to her house.

When he was settled at the table, she pulled deli meat out of the refrigerator, then grabbed some bread. He didn't have to know, but she was grateful for the company. In the last couple of weeks, she'd gotten used to having him around. Today, with him gone and the kids off playing with friends, the house had been too quiet.

"You never answered my question," he said. "Why do you stay here?"

"Because this is what I've always wanted."

"Roots?"

"Exactly. I like that it's boring. If I had my way, the rest of my life would be just as dull. You know, the Chinese have a saying—'May you live an interesting life.' Or is it live in interesting times? Either way, you get the point. I like the sameness, the traditions. My idea of happiness is serving exactly the same thing every year at Christmas. I like teaching the same curriculum each year at school. The kids are different and they learn at different rates. That's the challenge. But the rhythm is the same."

"Doesn't sound very exciting."

"I've had enough excitement to last me a lifetime. I grew up moving every year or two. I never made many friends. By the time I finally got in with some kids, it was time to move on." She remembered those times clearly. What she recalled most was always being lonely. "I never want my children to have to think about not fitting in. I want them to belong."

"I find it hard to believe you didn't always fit in."

"Why? You don't."

"How did you know that?"

His expression of surprise made her laugh out loud. "Mike, it's so obvious. You've never fit in. Look at how you're reacting to the suburbs, and this is about the most normal, most boring place in the world. You live on the fringes. Belonging gets in the way of what you do. Face it, a man comfortable with the rhythm of life doesn't choose to be a bodyguard."

She spread mustard on the bread, then folded several thin slices of roast beef. By now, she knew how he liked his sandwiches. She added extra lettuce without asking, and skipped the tomato.

"To answer the question you're thinking," she said as she set the plate in front of him, "the reason I know so much about you is that you're a lot like my dad. He didn't want to settle down, either. The only difference is that you're smart enough to do it on your own. He got married and dragged us along with him until we got to be too much of a burden. He loved the military and so did you.''

He took a bite of sandwich and chewed slowly. She grabbed two sodas and set one in front of him. After taking the seat across from his, she popped her can and took a swallow.

''The Marine Corps was the first place I fit in,'' he said. ''Sounds pretty sad, huh?''

''It makes perfect sense.'' Grace had told her a little about his childhood. By the time her friend had been born, Mike was nearly ten. He was always on the outside looking in, although he'd really cared about his baby half sister.

''I worked with the Military Police for a while, and I found out I was good at taking care of people. From there, I went to work for the Secret Service before going out on my own.''

''Do you ever think about doing anything else?''

He glanced down at his leg. ''It's been on my mind. I'm nearly forty. Everything's starting to go. The reflexes, timing.''

''Oh, yeah, you're so old. That's why all those women are chasing you.''

He didn't smile. ''It's a game for the young, Cindy. There aren't a lot of old bodyguards.''

''But you love the danger too much to give it up.''

''Maybe.'' He stared over her left shoulder, but she knew he was seeing something other than the kitchen. ''I spent my teenage years in trouble with the law. Now this is all I know. But taking a bullet has a way of making a man reevaluate what he wants to do with his life.''

''I can't see you sitting behind a desk.''

He grinned. "Me, neither."

She wondered what kind of man voluntarily faced death every day, then decided she didn't want to know. There was no point in getting emotionally involved. When he was healed, Mike would be moving on. She might see him from time to time when he came to visit Grace, if he ever did, but they could never have a relationship. If she forgot that, she was going to get hurt.

"I bet you did very well on jungle patrol," she said.

"Not bad."

She leaned forward. "Surviving in the jungle is a matter of blending in with the cover and adapting, right?"

"So?"

"I think that's your problem. You need to think of the suburbs as a different kind of jungle. You haven't been blending in and adapting. You need to get familiar with the territory and act like the natives. You need a cover."

He grinned. Her heart flopped over a couple of times in her chest. She ignored the sensation, along with the tingling that started in her toes and worked its way up. It was just a chill from the air conditioner or a rare summer malady she'd picked up somewhere. It wasn't Mike. She refused to be attracted to him. Okay, she wasn't going to lie to herself. She refused to be *more* attracted to him. It was bad enough that she couldn't stop thinking about their kiss. It haunted her and made her hunger for his touch.

She'd hoped it was just a general sort of awakening, a sign that she was finally ready to start dating. But her fantasies were specifically about Mike. Whenever she tried to picture herself in the arms of another man, the fantasy disappeared. Life was not fair.

"A cover," he said slowly, then nodded. "You're absolutely right. I've been doing this all wrong. I need to blend in." He drew his eyebrows together. "I've got the right car. God knows there are plenty of white Explorers here. But I don't have a family. That's a problem."

"You can borrow my kids."

His gaze locked with hers. "But that's not going to be enough, is it? I also need a wife, or at least a woman in my life. So what do you say, Cindy? This was your idea. You willing to see it through?"

"What are you asking?" Her voice was shaking and she didn't know why. Actually, she did know why—she just couldn't believe it!

"Will you pretend to be my girlfriend?"

Chapter Eight

Cindy parked in front of the mall. The two-story structure was all gleaming glass, with lush plants around the entrance and throughout the parking lot.

Mike eyed the building with distaste. Spending the afternoon shopping wasn't his idea of a good time, but Cindy had convinced him it was the quickest way to get the message out. According to her, everyone eventually ended up at the mall. He hoped those who spread rumors had decided to visit today.

He opened the passenger door and stepped out into the noon heat. It had rained the previous day and the humidity was unbearable. He'd worked in high temperatures before, but nothing like this. It might only be in the low nineties, but with the moisture in the air, he felt as if he were slowly being steamed alive, like a piece of broccoli.

"Can we go to the movies?" Allison asked as she scrambled from the back seat.

Cindy waited until all the doors were closed, then hit the alarm button on her key chain. The minivan chirped twice then was silent. "That's a good idea," she said.

"Not some dopey cartoon," Jonathan said. "Please, Mom, can we see that new action movie?"

Cindy brushed Jonathan's blond hair out of his eyes. "It's rated for adults only, so you know the answer to that, don't you?"

Jonathan turned to Mike. "Mike, you explain it to her. Sometimes it's important for a guy to do stuff, you know, like a man. Women don't understand that."

Mike stared at the kid. He was nine years old. Where did he hear that kind of talk? He grinned at the boy. "Mothers rule the world, kid. The sooner you learn that, the easier life will be."

"Ah, Mike." Jonathan scuffed his toe into the steamy blacktop.

Cindy leaned toward her son and got him in a head-lock. "I am your leader," she said, spacing the words out evenly and trying to sound like a machine. "You will obey me, or I will turn you into a toad."

Jonathan laughed up at her. The boy might look like his father, but he had his mother's good humor. "Ribit." They were still giggling when they reached the mall.

Mike held open the door. Allison skipped inside, followed by her brother. Cindy paused and glanced at Mike. "You can change your mind," she said.

"You're the one doing me a favor. If you want to back out, I'll understand."

She shook her head. "I've already agreed. If nothing else, it will be worth it to see the look on everyone's faces." Her green eyes danced with excitement.

A couple of days ago, those same eyes had widened with shock when he'd suggested she pose as his girlfriend to protect him. He'd been sort of shocked himself that he'd even asked. He hadn't planned it, but once he'd said the words, they made perfect sense. He hadn't expected Cindy to go along with it. After all, there wasn't anything in it for her. Much to his surprise, she had quickly agreed to the masquerade.

"You never told me why you're doing it," he said, waiting for her to precede him into the building.

She stepped inside and he followed her. "Number one, I owe Grace," she said, ticking off the reasons on her fingers. "Two, sometimes divorced women are treated as if they are invisible. I want to remind a few people that I'm still alive and well. Three, Nelson might find out and after what he's put me through, he deserves it. And four..." She smiled at him. Her dimple deepened. "I feel sorry for you. If you could have seen the panic in your eyes."

"Oh, gee, thanks. My ego needed a boost." With that, he put his arm around her.

Cindy stiffened. Her smile faded and she stared at him as if she'd never seen him before.

"Cindy?"

He started to lift his arm away. She blinked, then laughed and moved closer to him. "Momentary brain lapse. I forgot what we were doing here."

"But we were just talking about it."

"Talking and doing are not the same thing." A flush of color stained her cheeks. She gave him a tight smile, then glanced around. "Allison, Jonathan, you two stay within sight of us, remember?"

A chorus of "Yes, Mom" drifted back to them. Cindy turned to her right. Mike kept his arm around her and adjusted his limping stride to her shorter steps.

The interior of the mall was bright and open, with lush plants growing out of huge pots on the floor and hanging from beams in the glass ceiling. Most of the shoppers were women with children. About one out of two had strollers. Children were everywhere. Young kids running to store-window displays, then back to their mothers, teenagers collecting in groups and talking, babies sleeping or crying. Mike felt as if he were in some zoo specifically designed to study the raising of human young.

They'd gone along the bottom level a ways when he tightened his hold on Cindy's shoulders. "Just a minute. I want to look at the mall map."

"It's not necessary. We know our way around."

"I insist." He paused in front of the color-coded map and quickly got his bearings.

"Mike, I swear to you, we've been in every store. I could find my way around here blindfolded."

He released her and looked at the anchor stores. "I want to minimize our exposure. Tell me where we're going so I can plot our route."

His request was met with silence. He turned toward her. Allison and Jonathan were playing on a bench behind her. Mike didn't know the nature of the game, but it required them to circle the wooden seat, with a quick climb over the back every third or fourth trip.

She tilted her head. "Exposure to what?"

Danger. Undesirable elements. He looked around at the women shopping and their children. Not much danger here. Feeling slightly foolish, he shoved his hands into his shorts pockets. "Sorry. Force of habit."

"You might do better if you pretended to be enjoying yourself," she said. "You know, relax a little. Laugh, shop. You ever spend an hour just window-shopping?"

"Can't say that I have."

"It's an art form," she told him. "I'll try to teach it to you, but you have to give yourself up to the experience." She moved close and slipped her arm through his. Her skin was smooth and warm. He told himself the gesture was just part of the act, but she did it so easily, so unconsciously, he wanted to believe it was real.

Not real smart, Blackburne, he told himself. This situation was temporary. Cindy was helping him out of a rough spot, nothing more.

She leaned closer. Her left breast brushed against his upper arm. He felt the jolt clear to his groin and had to bite back a groan. "It would help if you tried to have a good time," she whispered.

"I'll try," he told her, then wondered how long it had been since he'd had fun just doing nothing. He'd been working nonstop for about three years. Before that—he shrugged. It was a lifetime ago. He didn't want to think about the past or the future. There was only today and the feel of Cindy so close to him.

They strolled down to the movie theater and had a lively debate over which show to see. Allison wanted to see a rerelease of a classic and Cindy agreed. Mike didn't care, so Jonathan was outvoted. He took it well, grumbling for a few minutes, then playing tag with Allison among the potted plants.

They walked slowly to the far end of the mall.

"How's your leg?" Cindy asked.

"Not bad. I eased up on the workout yesterday. Grace has a big Jacuzzi tub in her bathroom, and I've been using that every night. It helps."

"Let me know if you need the bandage changed."

The thought of her hands on his bare skin made him wish he was still bleeding. "I don't really need the bandage anymore. I'm just wearing it until the exit wound heals a little more. I don't want to gross everyone out."

"It's not that bad."

"You're used to it. I've seen the women around here checking out my leg."

She looked at him and raised her eyebrows. "Mike, they're not looking at your wound."

He didn't know what to say to that. Even worse, he could feel a faint heat on his cheeks. Hell, he hadn't blushed in years. "Yeah, well, I figure I can take off the bandage in a week or so."

"We'll have a coming-out party," she teased.

"Mommy, Mommy, look!" Allison stood in front of The Disney Store pointing to an animated display. The little girl had her nose plastered against the window. "Look, Mickey's waving." She waved back. "Hi, Mickey."

"I didn't know they had stores like this," Mike said.

"Everywhere. It's wonderful. They make buying for birthday parties very simple."

He felt a slight tugging on his free hand. Allison was pulling on him. "Come see, Mike. There's bookends I'm going to ask Santa for."

Cindy released him and he allowed the little girl to lead him into the store. In the front were racks of clothing— T-shirts, sweats, nightgowns, along with hats, ties and some odd-looking slippers. Halfway back, two large glass cases lined the walls. In between them were display shelves. Allison stopped in front of one and pointed.

"There," she said reverently.

The ceramic bookends were in two pieces. The right one showed Winnie the Pooh being pulled out of a hole by Christopher Robin. The left bookend was Pooh's back half, being pushed through the hole by Rabbit and Piglet and all Pooh's friends. The detail in the piece was amazing. Mike half expected the creatures to bounce to life.

"I didn't see them before my birthday," Allison told him, "so I'm going to ask Santa to bring them." She looked at him. "Do you think elves know how to make bookends?" she asked earnestly.

"Of course."

"Good." She smiled and curled her small hand around his. "Come see the stuffed animals." She pulled him to the back of the store and introduced him to all the creatures there. He hugged the ones she instructed him to, then spoke to a couple of others. She giggled when he snarled at the evil wizard doll.

The sound of her laughter was as welcome as desert rain. He liked Allison's being happy. It seemed to him in the last week or so, she'd started letting go of her imaginary friend.

"Where's Shelby?" he asked.

"She wanted to stay home," Allison answered easily. "Look, here's Pumba. He's a warthog."

By the time Cindy rescued him, he was well versed in the different characters. "Ask me anything," he said as they left the store. "I can recite plot lines, name characters and their offspring."

"You're very patient. I really appreciate that, and so do the children."

He shrugged. "It's no big deal. They're fun to be with." *You're fun to be with, too,* but he didn't say that. It would add a complication neither of them wanted.

"Mom, there's Kaleb and Brett. I want to go talk to them." Jonathan practically danced in place.

"Go," Cindy said. "But don't leave that spot."

She headed toward a bench in the shade of a large tree. When she sat down, Allison settled next to her and Mike took her other side. He put his arm around her. Just for show, he told himself, even as he noticed how well they fit together.

Cindy sighed. "I could live at the mall. Everything is new and clean. There's food so I wouldn't have to cook, movies and video games for the children and all the books I could possibly read."

Her hair brushed against his arm. He fingered a strand, noticing the softness and the way it felt against his skin. Without closing his eyes, he could imagine her straddling him, her head bent low as she—

"Mike, these are my friends, Kaleb and Brett." Jonathan grinned. "This is Mike. He's a bodyguard. He's been staying with us because he was shot, but he's getting better now."

Mike nodded at the two boys gaping at him. "Nice to meet you."

"Yeah," the larger of the two said. "You really a bodyguard?"

"That's right."

"You ever shoot anybody?"

"Yes, but only to protect a client."

"Wow, cool."

"Leave Mike alone," Cindy said. "He's resting." She dug in her purse and pulled out a handful of singles. "Go get an ice-cream cone." She looked at Mike. "You want one?"

He shook his head.

Allison jumped off the bench. "I want strawberry."

"I know, honey. Just tell the man." She indicated an ice-cream cart about fifteen feet away, across the open area. The four children made a mad dash to be first in line. Kaleb won, but he quickly relinquished his spot to Allison.

"Pcace at last," she said, leaning her head against his arm. Her eyes closed. "Tell me if they start to leave the area, please."

"I doubt they will. They're good kids."

"Thanks. I work at it. Although right now, all I want is to take a nap."

"Then I probably shouldn't tell you that Mary and Christina from the barbecue are heading this way."

Cindy straightened and her eyes snapped opened. "Where?" She followed where he pointed and sucked in a breath. The two women were standing in front of a shoe store studying a display. "They haven't seen us yet, but as soon as they do..." She angled toward him. "This is your big chance, Mike. Make it good."

From the tilt of her head, she was expecting a quick kiss on the cheek. He thought he'd cured her of that the last time they'd kissed. He touched his finger to her chin and turned her slightly, then bent forward and brushed his lips against hers.

Even as he reminded himself that they were in the middle of a mall and her children would probably see this, he had to fight the urge to deepen the kiss. Her lips were as warm and yielding as he remembered. He was instantly aroused. The situation wasn't helped by Cindy putting her hand on his upper arm and holding on as if she were in danger of blowing away.

He allowed himself to brush his tongue across her lower lip, then he pulled back. Her eyes were unfocused, her face flushed. "Good enough?"

"Extraordinary." Her voice was breathless.

"Me, too," he mumbled.

"What?" Before he had to answer, she glanced up and winced. "They saw us, that's for sure." She gave a little halfhearted wave.

Mike looked over his shoulder and saw the two women staring at them. When he smiled a greeting, they whispered to each other, then took off for the far end of the mall.

"It should take about an hour," Cindy said. "Beth is going to have fifteen messages on my phone by the time we get back. And is she going to be mad." She leaned against the bench. "Beth can keep a secret, so if you don't mind, I want to tell her the truth."

"Fine, but if she asks if you saw me naked, be sure and tell her yes."

"Should I tell her I was impressed?"

"You have to ask?"

Her laughter warmed him like summer sunshine. In that moment, he forgot that her children and their friends were eating ice cream not fifteen feet away. He forgot about the people shopping around them and the fact that Cindy wasn't for him. He wanted her. He could handle the need. What scared him was that he also wanted to *be* with her. It wasn't just about sex and he didn't know how to deal with that.

Lucky for both of them, Cindy wasn't the type to have a meaningless affair, because he had the feeling it *would* mean something and then where would he be?

A few minutes later, they made their way to the movies. Jonathan grumbled a few times about the cartoon, but he was soon engrossed in the story. The boy sat between Mike and Cindy, with Allison on Mike's other side. Probably better that way, Mike thought, knowing how the darkness would have tempted him.

When the evil trees closed in on the beautiful princess, Allison whimpered in fear. Without thinking, he gathered her up onto his lap. She buried her head in his shoulder and whispered for him to tell her when the scary part was over.

She was small and slight. As he held the child, he wondered how something so fragile could survive. She smelled of summer and strawberries. Her hands were sticky on his arms, but he didn't mind.

At last the princess made it out of danger. He whispered that it was safe to look. Allison twisted around to face the movie screen but she didn't slide off his lap and Mike found he didn't want to make her.

Further into the film, the princess kissed her prince. Jonathan groaned and covered his eyes. "Yuck," he said quietly. "I hate this part."

Mike chuckled, then looked at Cindy. She was smiling at him. He felt the connection, the circle of family. For the first time in his life, he was inside where it was warm.

Mike pitched the ball. The batter swung and missed. Jonathan called out for him to pay more attention to the ball.

Cindy stepped back from the window and reached for the pitcher of brewed tea. She poured the dark liquid into two glasses full of ice, then carried them both to the table.

Beth poured a package of artificial sweetener into hers, then took a sip. "How long does this game of pretend go on?"

"For as long as he's here. If everyone thinks we're a couple, Mike is safe."

"I understand what Mike gets out of it, but what about you?"

"I'm doing it for Grace," Cindy said, sitting down opposite her friend. "I owe her. And for Mike. He's a nice guy."

"He's a little more than that."

"I don't know what you mean."

"Uh-huh, sure."

Cindy didn't dare glance at Beth. She didn't want to see the knowing expression on her friend's face. Beth had brought up an interesting point. Why *was* Cindy helping Mike out?

She was doing it for the reasons she'd told Beth and for one other. She was doing it because she liked pretending it was real. She liked the closeness they shared, she liked him touching her and being able to touch him back. Being with him made her remember all the good parts about being married. Being with him made her feel alive. It was the safest way to get what she wanted. Mike was leaving. She knew that in advance. She wouldn't be foolish enough to give her heart away, so she wouldn't have to worry about getting it broken.

"So, have you seen him naked?" Beth asked teasingly.

Cindy had known the question was coming. She'd even prepared a witty answer. But instead of saying that, she slapped her hands down on the table. "Dammit, there's more to a relationship than sex."

Beth stared at her, then took a sip of tea. "Honey, you're not falling for him, are you?"

She'd surprised herself with her outburst. "Of course not. That would be crazy. We're just friends. Mike is . . ."

"Handsome?" Beth offered helpfully.

"Well, yes."

"Funny?"

She smiled. "Very."

"Charming?"

"When he wants to be."

"Single?"

"Obviously." Cindy frowned. "What's your point?"

"I don't have one." Beth folded the empty sweetener packet in half. "As long as you're sure you're not falling for him. It seems to me it would be very easy for this game of pretend to get out of hand."

"I'm not going to let that happen," Cindy said. "He's not my type."

"In the two years you've been single, you haven't had one date. I don't think you're qualified to know what your type is."

"Maybe not, but whatever my type is, Mike isn't it. The man can fit his belongings into two duffel bags. I want someone who's going to stick around. Someone stable. With roots."

"You had that with Nelson, and he still left you."

"Thanks for reminding me."

Beth leaned forward. Her blue eyes darkened with sympathy. "You know what I'm saying. You thought Nelson would be a sure thing, and he wasn't. You assume Mike is wrong for you. Maybe he is wrong. And just maybe he's Mr. Right. You can handle this any way you like. But like I said, this game of pretending to have a relationship could get out of hand. What if you stop pretending, but he still thinks it's a game? I don't want you getting hurt."

"That won't happen. I'd be crazy to fall for a guy like him."

Beth stood up. "Sounds like you're trying to convince yourself more than me," she said, then left.

Cindy sat at the kitchen table a long time. She thought about what her friend had said. It was a risk. She would be the first to admit that something about Mike got to her. It wasn't just his good looks. It was the way he took the time to be with her kids, and his kindness. Okay, and maybe it was the way he turned her on.

The back door opened. Five sweaty children and one sweaty adult spilled into the kitchen.

"We're thirsty," Jonathan said.

She pulled out a pitcher of lemonade from the fridge as her son set out plastic glasses. Mike limped over to the kitchen table and sat down. "They're thirsty. I'm going to have a heart attack. Do you know how hot it is out there?"

The five boys collected their cups and started to leave. "You coming, Mike?" Jonathan asked.

"No," he gasped, and leaned back in the chair. "I can't keep up."

Jonathan laughed and closed the door behind him.

"You have to be careful in this heat," Cindy told him, eyeing his damp T-shirt.

"I know. I still don't have my endurance. The leg is healing, but it's going to be a while."

He took the glass she offered and downed the lemonade in three big gulps. As he handed it back to her, he grabbed the hem of his T-shirt and raised it to wipe his face. She had a brief glimpse of his hard, muscled belly and chest. His bare skin gleamed from sweat. She'd seen his chest several times while he'd been sick. She'd always admired it, but it was only recently that the sight of it sent her heart into overdrive. She supposed it was because when he was a patient, she'd thought of him as someone she had to take care of and now she thought of him as a man.

She poured him another glass of lemonade. "Did you have fun?"

"Yeah."

"Don't sound so surprised."

"I can't help it. I'm discovering a whole new species of humans. Kids are pretty cool."

"Don't let them fool you," she said. "They can be a real pain sometimes."

"I know that." He took a drink, then set the glass on the table.

"You'd be a good father," she said, putting the now-empty pitcher in the sink.

She glanced at Mike. He raised his eyebrows and shook his head.

"You don't agree?" she asked.

"No. I would be pretty good being a part-time parent, but I doubt if I could be there for the long haul. Besides, I'm just a beat-up, scarred, slightly over-the-hill body-guard. Who would want me?"

He took another drink and closed his eyes as if not really expecting an answer. Cindy thought about how he made her feel when he held her, and how good he was with the kids. She rinsed out the pitcher and started to make another batch of lemonade, all the while the answer to his question echoing silently inside her head.

Who would want a beat-up, scarred, slightly over-the-hill bodyguard? She might.

Chapter Nine

The crash of thunder echoed through the house. Mike sat upstairs in the game room, watching the bolts of lightning filling the sky. Rain pounded against the windows. According to the weather channel on television, the storm was going to be a bad one, lasting most of the afternoon. He stretched out on the sofa, propped his feet on the coffee table and prepared to enjoy the show.

The wound in this thigh had almost healed. He'd been working out regularly at the country club, but never on weekends. His strength was returning, although his endurance was going to take a little longer to reach one hundred percent. It was a slow process, but he was improving daily. That's what he'd come to Sugar Land to do.

He glanced at the clock above the entertainment center. It was late Saturday afternoon. He'd begun to measure his life in two-week increments. The beginning and ending of each time period was Jonathan and Allison spending the weekend with their father. They'd left that morning.

He didn't see them every day, but he still missed them when they were gone. At least every other day, they came over and invited him to play in the greenbelt or go to lunch or a movie with them. The invitations rarely came from Cindy and he wasn't sure if she liked his tagging along or not. She always seemed pleased to see him. If she'd been one of his usual women, he would have known exactly what she was thinking. If she'd been one of his usual women, he wouldn't have cared as much.

In the last few weeks, he'd begun depending on her less. The grocery store was no longer strange. He'd gotten used to everyone's knowing who he was. Since word had spread that he and Cindy were an item, the illicit invitations had slowed. He was grateful, but he sometimes wondered what would happen to Cindy when he was gone. Would everyone assume she'd been dumped? He hadn't thought that far ahead when he'd asked her to pretend to be involved with him. She hadn't mentioned it, but that didn't mean there weren't ramifications for her.

A bolt of lightning hit the ground close to the house. The instantaneous explosion of thunder shook the windows. He rose to his feet and walked downstairs. His limp was barely noticeable. He crossed the kitchen and stared out the window at Cindy's house. From this side he couldn't see anything but her fence and front yard. For all he knew, she was gone. Or entertaining.

He grimaced, not wanting to think about her being with another man. Why wouldn't she be? She was bright, pretty, sexy as hell. Unless all the single men in the area were blind, someone had to have noticed her.

With her pretending to be involved with him, he knew it was illogical to assume she had a man in her house, but once the thought was planted, he couldn't let it go. He wanted to walk over and find out, but he couldn't think of a good enough excuse.

Besides, it wasn't his business. She was just a friend, nothing more. What she did with her personal life was her business. And even if it were his business, he didn't want to get involved. Bad enough that he was already attached to her kids; he wasn't going to make it worse by becoming attached to the lady herself.

That decided, he opened the refrigerator. It was too early for dinner, but maybe he could figure out what he was going to have. He'd finished his stash of frozen dinners. He could go to the market again. Or maybe a movie. He needed to get out.

The next bolt of lightning didn't hit close to the house, nor was the accompanying thunder particularly loud, but even as the sound rumbled through the afternoon, the lights in the house faded and the air conditioner stopped.

He stood in the center of the kitchen waiting for the electricity to be restored. It often went out for a few seconds during storms. After two minutes, he figured it wasn't going to be coming back on anytime soon. Maybe he should go and make sure Cindy was all right.

It was, he acknowledged as he dashed through the rain, a flimsy excuse. Cindy had been surviving storms long before he arrived in town. But it was the best he could come up with under the circumstances. Admitting that he simply wanted to see her wasn't an option.

He ran across her lawn and down the driveway. Once under the protection of the breezeway, he slowed, then stopped in front of her back door and knocked.

"Come in," she called.

He opened the door and stepped inside.

Her house was cool, dark and silent. There were no lights, no hum of the air conditioner or ceiling fans. "Where are you?" he asked.

"In the living room."

He crossed the family room floor and entered the large open living area. The ceiling was two stories high, the windows nearly that tall. Outside, bushes and crepe myrtle trees swayed in the wind. Cindy was sitting in one corner of the sofa that faced the window. She'd pulled her knees up to her chest. Her shoulder-length hair was loose around her face.

He stopped in front of her and glared. "You shouldn't leave your back door open and you shouldn't just call 'Come in.' What if I'd been a burglar?"

She glanced up at him. Her eyes were a mossy green in the dark gray of the afternoon light, her face pale and devoid of makeup. She wore a white short-sleeved shirt that buttoned up the front and pull-on shorts.

"Only my friends use the back door," she said. "Burglars don't knock and strangers come to the front."

"You should be more careful."

"Yes, Mike. I'll do my best." She leaned her head back against the sofa and closed her eyes.

"You okay?" he asked.

"Fine."

"The electricity is out. I came by to make sure everything was all right."

"Couldn't be better. I love summer storms." She waved one arm toward the far end of the sofa. "Have a seat. Do you want some wine?"

"Sure."

He moved around the light oak coffee table and sat down. Lightning lit the sky like a strobe light. Thunder was one long continuous boom. Cindy rose to her feet and collected a few fat candles from the mantel. She set them on the coffee table and lit them. The flickering lights added a soft glow to the room.

When she returned from the kitchen, she was carrying a bottle of red wine, a corkscrew and two glasses. Mike took the bottle from her and opened it. She settled on the sofa, staying in the far corner, but angling toward him.

"To summer," she said, taking the glass he offered.

"To summer." Their voices were quiet in the still room, the sound of the clinking glass unnaturally loud.

She sipped the dark liquid, then sighed. "Lovely. I hope the electricity stays out for another hour. Just long enough for us to enjoy the quiet, but not so long that the frozen foods spoil."

Mike grinned. "Ever practical."

"I'm a mother. I have to be."

She took another drink, then leaned forward and set the glass on the table. The front of her blouse gaped slightly. He had a brief impression of pale curves and white lace, then she straightened.

"I haven't seen you in a couple of days," she said. "What have you been doing?"

"Working out. I seem to be collecting a smaller audience each time."

"But you still have that core group of devoted fans."

"Don't remind me." He took a drink of his wine. The taste was smooth with a hint of a bite. Very nice. "I've been catching up on my reading. Trying to avoid television. Do you know what's on during the day?" He shuddered. "I can't believe people go on talk shows and admit all these personal problems to millions of viewers. And the soaps. Thank God for CNN."

"And sports."

"That, too."

The wind shifted so the rain pelted the tall windows. There were three across the back of the living room. Two slender windows on either side of a wide one in the center. The curtains had been drawn back, the lace sheers pushed aside.

Cindy leaned forward. "Isn't it beautiful?"

"Yes." He watched jagged flashes cut through the gray clouds. "I didn't realize the weather changed so much here in Houston."

"It's never boring, that's for sure." She gave him a quick smile, then turned her attention back to the storm. "Fronts come through quickly. In the winter it can go from sixty-five to below forty degrees in about fifteen minutes. You can run the air conditioner in the morning and the heater that night."

"I can't believe you ever use the heater," he said.

"It is a little warm right now."

"Warm? I've been in saunas that are cooler than this."

"It will be cool right now, in the rain, but as soon as the storm passes, it will get muggy. But it gets hot back East and in Los Angeles in the summer."

"Not like this." He took another sip of wine, then leaned back on the sofa, resting the glass on his belly. "L.A. is a dry heat and it comes and goes in cycles. New York has humidity, but nothing like this. I spent some time in Singapore during the summer. Now *that's* heat."

She turned toward him. "Where else have you been?"

He shrugged. "Everywhere. It all blurs after a while. You traveled a lot, too, when you were a kid."

"Not like that. It was military bases and mostly in the States. We never went anywhere fun. That might have made up for moving all the time. If I had my wish, I would never move again."

He glanced around the room. "It's very nice here."

"Thanks. I like it. When I was growing up, I used to think about the house I would buy when I was an adult. I used to plan the rooms and how I would decorate them."

"How close did you come?"

She picked up her wine and chuckled. "Fortunately, I modified my plans as I got older. I can't remember what I would have chosen when I was Allison's age, but I'm sure it would have been awful." She took a sip, then continued, "I always wanted my home to be welcoming. The sort of place someone would want to stay."

"Then you've accomplished your goal." He'd felt welcome in her house from the first moment he regained consciousness. Now, with a storm raging outside, the house felt like a haven.

"Thanks. I'd like to redo this room." She patted the floral-print sofa. "Maybe get rid of those drapes. I don't like the gray. It's a little cold for me, but Nelson liked it. I've changed the bedroom since he left and I'd like to do more, but it has to be slow. I'm still trying to make it on a teacher's salary."

She leaned toward the coffee table and set down her wine. As she shifted back in place, she moved closer. Mike told himself it was a completely unconscious action. Cindy considered him a friend. She was relaxed around him. She wasn't coming on to him.

But his body didn't want to listen to logic. From the moment he'd first seen her, he'd thought she was attractive. If he recalled those first few foggy minutes correctly, he'd thought she was a naked angel sent to him from heaven. Now he knew she was even better than that, she was a flesh-and-blood woman. And he wanted her.

He rested his head on the sofa and sipped his wine, all the while listening to her plans about wallpaper and new carpeting. He enjoyed the sound of her voice. It nearly blocked out the blood roaring through his veins. His skin was hot, his groin hard. Just being with her turned him on. He didn't want to think about what would happen if they actually touched. Or kissed. Or made love.

He had a bad feeling it would be pretty damn good—and a complete disaster. He wasn't into commitments and Cindy didn't know any other way to do it. So they would be friends, and when he left here late this afternoon, he would take a cold shower and think pure thoughts.

"Mike! You're not listening to me."

"Sorry. Men are genetically predisposed not to be able to talk about decorating."

"That's not true." She gave him a mocking glare. "Men very much want to live in a nice house, but many of them don't want to be bothered with doing any of the work required to get it that way."

"That, too," he admitted. He finished his wine and sat up to put the empty glass on the table. When he settled on the sofa again, he turned toward her. They were definitely closer to each other now. Each of them had about eight inches of space behind them, and less than that between them. Cindy was shaking her head. She hadn't noticed. He wondered if she would.

"I don't know how you stand not having a home," she said.

"You get used to it."

"I never did."

"You never wanted to."

She sat on her right hip, with her knee nearly touching his thigh and her body resting against the sofa. "What's so great about having nowhere to belong?"

"I wasn't like you, Cindy. I was a bad kid."

"What makes you think I was a good one?"

He reached out his hand and touched the tip of her nose. "I can see it in your eyes. You sat in the front of the classroom, did your homework every day and got good grades."

"You were the bad boy in the back of the room. You annoyed the teacher with your smart remarks and tempted the girls with your smoldering eyes."

Was she tempted? The heat inside him begged him to find out. What kept him in check was the fact that he liked Cindy, and she deserved a hell of a lot better than him.

"I stole cars," he said.

She didn't act surprised. "Did you go to prison?"

"Aren't you shocked?"

"You once mentioned your being on the wrong side of the law when you were a teenager. No one ends up where you are by taking an ordinary path."

She was smart. He liked that about her. "I was given the choice between prison and the military. I decided on the military, the judge picked the marines. Looking back, I suppose he figured they'd either straighten me out or kill me."

"And here you are."

"I know now that I just wanted attention. My mother had remarried and started a second family. She never cared what I did, anyway, so it was easy to run the streets. But I got caught." He drew in a deep breath and let it out.

"Why a bodyguard?" she asked. "There are a lot of other kinds of security jobs."

"I don't have a death wish. That's what some people think. It's not about the dying, it's about being better. When a client hires me, he's usually been threatened. My job is to be smarter and faster than the enemy. Think like him, know him, then beat him. If I do my job right, no one gets hurt. If I don't, someone dies. Those are about the highest stakes around. Every situation is different, but the enemy is constant.''

She'd tilted her head in that way that told him she was pondering something. ''What are you thinking?'' he asked.

''You might not have a death wish, but you are willing to die. What makes you offer that sacrifice?''

''I don't think of it like that. Death is just another way of finding out I didn't do my job right.''

She leaned forward. Her hair swung down against her cheek and she brushed it back impatiently. ''That's why you don't have a place, isn't it? Caring about something, belonging, makes it too difficult to accept that ultimate price. Or do you think that's what you deserve? Is it a punishment? What are you paying for, Mike?''

Her gaze was intense, all her attention focused on him. He stirred restlessly on the sofa, not knowing how to answer her. She'd strayed dangerously close to the truth he'd always tried to hide, even from himself. The specter of not being good enough had haunted him from childhood. He'd always believed the reason he'd been emotionally abandoned by his mother was that there was a problem with him. His stepfather's ambivalence had reinforced that idea. Women came and went in his life with a regularity that convinced him they could all see the truth. It wasn't them, it was him. A flaw he couldn't hide or fix. Once he realized he lacked whatever made a person lovable, he made sure he was in a situation where love was impractical. It was easier than facing the reality of his own shortcomings. So much for hiding behind a facade of confidence. Cindy had seen right through him.

''I'm sorry,'' she said, and touched his forearm. ''I've had just enough psychology to spout nonsense. I didn't mean to offend you.''

"I'm not offended," he said, wondering how she'd seen the truth so quickly. He felt exposed, as if he'd walked into a formal event completely naked.

"How long can you keep on doing it?" she asked. "Where do old bodyguards go?"

"I don't ask that question. This is all I know."

"Are there security jobs available?"

"Sure. Some companies hire bodyguards to train executives to protect themselves, especially when they travel overseas."

"You'd be good at that."

"Why?"

She smiled. "You're very patient with the children. That's the mark of a good teacher. Trust me on this, I'm an expert."

Her fingers still rested on his arm. Her casual exposure of his greatest weakness had destroyed his desire as effectively as sunlight burns a worm. But her equally casual acceptance of the flaw allowed him to breathe normally and stay in his seat. Gradually, her touch soothed him.

She drew her hand back to her lap. "Of course, if you took a different kind of job, you wouldn't be able to seduce women so easily."

He laughed out loud. "Is that what you think I do?"

"Don't expect me to believe that you haven't used your job to get sex. I've seen what's happened here. The bodyguard thing really pushes some female buttons. I think it's because we assume you can take care of us."

He wondered if she really meant "us," as in she was attracted to him, too.

"So, have you?" She blushed.

"Now you sound like Beth."

"And you're avoiding the question."

"Yes, I've used my job to get women, but not often."

She scrambled into a kneeling position, then sank back until she was sitting on her ankles. "Really? What's it like?"

"For one thing, most women don't ask so many questions."

"But you're not interested in having sex with me," she said with a dismissive wave of her hand. "Come on. Tell me what they ask or say."

"They want to know about the glamour, the celebrities."

She wrinkled her nose. "That's boring."

He shook his head. "You're not like those women. Maybe that's why I'm having such a hard time fitting in here. My job is based on predicting other people's actions before even they know what they're going to do. Here I'm completely at a loss."

"You don't understand our world, so how can you predict us?"

"Excellent point. For a girl."

"Now *you* sound like Jonathan."

He smiled, then he leaned against the sofa back and studied her. "I understand criminals better than suburban women and children."

"Isn't that an interesting comment on the 'burbs? And here I thought we were so normal."

She laughed. The corners of her eyes crinkled. The lightning had passed, but rain continued to splatter against the windows. The electricity hadn't come back on. The afternoon was still gray and dark, with the only light coming from the candles flickering on the coffee table.

"You're very beautiful," he said without thinking.

Her laughter faded into a rueful smile. "I wish that were true."

"Why would I lie?"

"Because you're a nice guy."

"No one's ever accused me of that before."

"You're nice to my kids and to me. You make me feel good about myself." She tugged on her shorts. "Look at me. I didn't even put on makeup or get dressed up this morning, and Nelson actually came to the door. For the first time, I didn't care what he thought of me. I didn't mind that Hilari is four inches taller and twenty pounds lighter than I am. You're right. Nelson was a fool for leaving me. I probably should have figured that out a while ago, but I didn't until you mentioned it. I'm really grateful for that."

"Funny, I don't want your gratitude." She saw him as some damn do-gooder.

She straightened. "Did I say something wrong?"

"No. It's not you. It's just—hell . . ."

He reached forward and grabbed her upper arms. If she'd protested or resisted in the slightest, he would have let her go. But she watched mutely as he drew her closer. He lowered his mouth to hers. Her eyes fluttered closed and she breathed his name.

Even as he touched her lips, he told himself it was a mistake. He couldn't get involved with her or make promises. He didn't know how, and he refused to lie to her or lead her on. Which made kissing her a mistake. But when her arms came around the back of his neck, he knew he would pay whatever price this moment cost. She was worth it all.

Her mouth was soft and yielding. She tasted sweet. Still holding her arms, he shifted and lowered them both to the sofa. They pressed together from shoulder to knees, their legs tangled, their torsos brushing. Her arms held him close as if she feared he would escape. If he hadn't been so busy relearning every millimeter of her delicious mouth, he would have told her there was nowhere else he would rather be . . . except possibly in her bed.

Her fingers combed through his hair, sending shivers down his spine. He'd mentioned getting it cut, but she'd teased him about being afraid of looking normal. He loved the feel of her nails stroking his scalp and her palms massaging his neck. In that moment, he resolved to never cut his hair again.

As his mouth pressed against hers, he slipped his hands down her spine. He could feel her warm skin and the tempting fastener of her bra. He lingered there as if he could unhook it by will alone. She felt delicate and fragile against him. He could nearly span her back with a splayed hand. She was soft where he was hard, as if their bodies had been specifically designed for this moment.

She moaned impatiently, then squirmed against him. Her mouth parted. He tried to resist the temptation, touching his tongue to her lower lip before slipping inside. But her heat beckoned and he didn't have the strength to deny her or himself. He moved into her mouth.

The contrast of textures delighted him, her quivering response, the brush of her tongue against his, sent blood surging through his body before pooling in his groin. His erection flexed inside his shorts. She arched her hips toward him as if she'd felt it and wanted more.

He angled his head, seeking all of her mouth. They touched, moist heat to moist heat. Over and around, again and again, until his breathing was rapid and his body hot with longing. She moved her legs against his. Her smooth skin taunted him with images of her naked beneath him, her long legs wrapped around his hips as she drew him in fully. The picture was so real, the feeling so intense, he had to fight the need to explode right then.

He grabbed her hips and shifted, drawing her on top of him. She straddled him. Instantly, her feminine heat surrounded his groin. He caught his breath.

"That might have been a mistake," he murmured against her mouth.

She laughed. "What *are* you hiding in your pocket?"

He kept his hands on her hips, urging her to rock against him. It was the sweet kind of torture. He grimaced, then stilled her.

"If you knew what you did to me," he said.

She rocked once more. He sucked in a breath. "I have a fair idea," she told him. Her smile faded. "You do the same. Every part of me is on fire."

Her confession was nearly as arousing as her actions had been. He wrapped his arms around her back and drew her down until her breasts pressed against his chest. His mouth opened and she plunged inside, taking him as he'd taken her.

He moved his hands lower, down her back to the curve of her hips. Sliding up, he slipped his fingers under the hem of her shorts and touched the backs of her legs. The skin was silky smooth. She whimpered.

Closing his lips around her tongue, he suckled gently. Her thighs tightened. He moved his hands back up her hips and her waist, to her ribs. Still he held her captive in his mouth. Her pelvis began to move against his. He forced himself not to notice, then cupped her breasts.

She froze in place as if every part of her focused on his touch. She filled his hands. He could feel the tautness of her nipples through her shirt and bra. He circled his palms against the tight buds and made her shudder.

Even as his fingers learned her curves, he moved his head and kissed her jaw, her ear, then nibbled on her neck. Her breathing was rapid pants, but then so was his.

His blood bubbled and boiled, his groin throbbed in time with the rapid cadence of his heart. It would have been easy to pull her shorts off and push his down. Too damn easy.

He moved her next to him, then turned on his side. One by one he unfastened the buttons on her shirt. She made it difficult by kissing his face and sticking her tongue in his ear. He laughed softly.

"I like to hear you laugh," she murmured. "You don't do it enough."

"You wear too many clothes." He pulled her shirt free of her shorts and stared down at her lacy bra. Her full breasts strained against their confinement. He could see her pale skin and the deep rose of her nipples.

"Touch me," she whispered.

Her green eyes were dark with desire, her mouth swollen from his kisses. He'd never seen anything so lovely in his life. He'd never wanted a woman as much. They were both adults. They knew what they were doing.

Even as his fingers touched her breast and his thumb traced her nipple, he knew he was lying. Cindy was reacting, not thinking. He would be willing to bet his next job that she hadn't been with a man since Nelson left. Mike wasn't sure he wanted that kind of responsibility.

"Yes," she breathed as he rubbed the sensitive tip.

He also wasn't sure he could resist her. He wasn't anybody's idea of a hero. Why couldn't he just take what she offered and forget about the consequences? They'd never bothered him before.

"I want you," he said.

Her eyes fluttered closed, and she arched her breasts toward him.

He reached behind her for the hook to her bra. As his fingers fumbled with the fastener, the electricity came back on.

Instantly, light flooded the room. The refrigerator began to hum and the air conditioner kicked in.

"Talk about getting a sign from above," he said and drew his hand away.

She stared at him. "You're not stopping?"

"We both know I'm the wrong guy for you."

"Of course, but..." She drew in a deep breath and let it go slowly. "I can't believe you're being sensible about this."

He smiled regretfully and pushed up off the sofa. "I can't believe I am, either." He held out his hand. She placed her fingers against his and he helped her to her feet.

Her hair was tousled, her face flushed. Worse, her shirt was open and he could see her perfect breasts. The painful throbbing in his groin reminded him he was going to regret this act of nobility for a long time.

"I'm sorry," he said. "I had no right to start anything."

"I don't know if you did or not. Isn't that interesting? I do know you're all wrong for me, so it really is best that we stopped." She pulled the ends of her shirt together and started fastening the buttons. "I have a favor to ask. Could you please be a little less attractive next time? Maybe even act surly around me or the kids."

"I'll do my best."

She tucked her shirt into her shorts and glanced at him. "Still friends?"

The desire had faded from her eyes, leaving behind embarrassment. She was bluffing her way through. He hated that he'd made her self-conscious. "Always," he promised. "Cindy, I'm really sorry."

She held up a hand. "You have nothing to apologize for. It was bound to happen. We spend a lot of time together, we like each other. No big deal. I can handle this. Really."

"Then I'll see you soon," he said, walking toward the back door.

Her smile was tight. He wanted to say something, anything, to make her feel better, but he couldn't find the words. Soon he would be gone and she would forget him.

He wouldn't forget her, though. She was the first time he'd ever thought about staying.

Chapter Ten

Cindy sat at the kitchen table staring at her piles of coupons. Tomorrow was double-coupon day at the market, and she wanted to take advantage of the savings. But figuring out what on earth she could make with a half-price can of olives even though none of them really liked olives wasn't the challenge it used to be. She was distracted.

She leaned back in her chair and glanced out the kitchen window. She could see the greenbelt and her children playing. One of the fathers had built a playhouse. They couldn't leave it out all the time, but the family dragged it out on weekends. A herd of children was playing some elaborate game. The summer heat didn't seem to bother the kids. Cindy admired their endurance and their enthusiasm. She was barely getting by.

It was all Mike's fault.

She'd been doing fine until a week ago. Until a summer storm had brought him to her door. She'd been able to deal with her own ridiculous fantasies about him because she knew they were just daydreams without a chance of coming true. She'd had a crush on him, had even imagined what it would be like to make love with him. The fantasy had been wonderful. Unfortunately, the reality was even better.

Even thinking about his kisses or the feel of his hands on her skin made her tremble. She tried to tell herself she was reacting to the fact that she hadn't been with a man since before Nelson had left. And the last year of their marriage hadn't been very physical. So naturally she'd responded to the sexual advances of an attractive man she admired. But in her heart she knew it was more than that. When she and Nelson had made love, she'd been satisfied. Okay, maybe the earth didn't move, but she understood the workings of her body and she knew she'd achieved physical release. She enjoyed the process, but it hadn't haunted her.

She couldn't put those moments with Mike out of her mind. When she least expected them or wanted them to appear, the memories were there. Talking to friends, reading bedtime stories to her children, doing laundry. She would blink, and suddenly she could feel his strong hands on her body. Her breasts grew heavy, her thighs trembled and she was ready for him. Only he wasn't anywhere around.

What made it worse was that Mike was able to put the situation out of *his* mind. Not by a word or a look did he even hint at how close they'd come to crossing the line. After his initial apology, he hadn't said a word on the subject. Nor did he avoid her. He was friendly, considerate, great with her kids and exactly like a big brother to her. She couldn't ask for a better neighbor. She was getting everything she wanted; she should be thrilled.

So why couldn't she concentrate on her coupons? Why did she continually glance out the window hoping to catch a glimpse of Mike? He'd left on a jog just a few minutes ago. He wouldn't return for an hour. But she kept checking, hoping he would come back with a skinned knee or something that would require her services. What kind of person hoped someone would get injured just so she could be close to him and touch him for a few minutes? She was definitely messed up.

"Stop thinking about him," she commanded herself.

It was good advice. Mike was going to get better and leave. As they'd both agreed, he was completely wrong for her. Bodyguards don't get off work every day at five. That's what she wanted. Someone stable, someone she could count on. There were no promises in life, but she wanted the next best alternative—she wanted a sure thing. Mike Blackburne was a wonderful man, but he didn't come with guarantees.

Before she could scold herself for continuing to think about him, the phone rang. She gratefully abandoned her coupons and picked up the receiver.

"Hello?"

"Cindy, it's Grace. Where's my big brother? He's not picking up at the house." Like the last time Grace had called, the connection from Hong Kong was amazingly clear.

Cindy laughed and took the cordless receiver back to her seat at the table. "Mike is fine. He's out jogging."

"Jogging? Is he nuts? It's got to be a million degrees there, now. It's July, for heaven's sake."

"A million and ten degrees. He swears he's acclimating." She glanced at the clock over the oven. "He just left, so he won't be back for about an hour."

"Oh, no, he's trying to kill himself."

"Grace, he's doing great. The reason he's gone so long is that he jogs really slow. I mean, Allison can run faster than him. The bullet wound is healing well, he's been working out, he's getting stronger. Your brother is fine."

"Oh?" Grace's voice was questioning. "Fine as in healthy, or fine as in 'what a fine specimen of a man'?"

"Healthy. He's perfectly healthy."

"You have to admit he's very handsome."

He was handsome. So handsome it drove her nuts, but no, she didn't have to admit it. "How's Hong Kong?"

"Wonderful. Don't try to change the subject." Grace paused for a moment. "I've heard you two are an item."

Cindy propped her elbows on the table and rested her forehead in her hands. "We're pretending to be an item. Women here were coming on to him. You know how it is. He didn't know what to do, so we decided to throw everyone off the trail by getting word out that we were dating. I'm just trying to be a good neighbor."

"Uh-huh. So that's why he kissed you when you were at the mall?"

Cindy didn't swear much, but she was sure thinking about starting. "I can't believe you heard about that."

"I received two letters and one phone call on the subject. So it's true?"

"Yes, he kissed me, but it was just because we wanted people to think we were a couple. If you heard about it, it obviously worked."

"So there's nothing romantic between you?"

"I swear." Cindy made an X over her heart. There wasn't anything romantic between Mike and her. That didn't mean she wasn't tempted, or didn't have her daydreams.

"And you've never kissed any other time?"

That she wasn't willing to swear to. "Grace, you're looking for something that doesn't exist. Mike is a great guy. I like him, the kids think the world of him and I'm thrilled to be able to pay you back for all that you've done for me. But I'm not having a relationship with your brother. We aren't right for each other."

Grace sighed. "I know. I was just hoping for a miracle. Mike's nearly forty. He can't run around after bad guys forever. I just want him to be happy, and I thought maybe you would be the one to help him see it was time to settle down. You guys would be great together."

Cindy didn't want to think about that. Being great with Mike was a guaranteed ticket to heartbreak. She didn't need the problem, despite the temptation.

"Can we please talk about something else?" Cindy asked.

"Sure." Grace chattered about her travels in Hong Kong and all the wonderful silks she'd bought. Cindy brought her up-to-date on the happenings in the neighborhood.

After a few minutes, Grace sighed. "I've got to go. I've limited my phone-call time to two hours a month and I've just used up nearly a quarter of that. Give Mike a kiss for me."

"Grace!"

"On the cheek. You're so suspicious. Take care of yourself, too. I miss you."

"I miss you, too. Bye."

She hit the off button and set the portable receiver on the table. She wanted her friend back, but before Grace returned, Mike would leave. It was an interesting dilemma.

The phone rang again. Cindy grinned. No doubt Grace had just one more thing to tell her.

"Hello?"

"Cindy, I need to talk about Allison."

Her smile faded and with it, her good humor. The voice was familiar. A few months ago, just hearing it would put her stomach in knots, but that had passed. Now she felt nothing but mild annoyance at the interruption. She glanced out the window and saw her daughter laughing with her friends.

"What's the problem, Nelson?" she asked coolly, knowing exactly why her ex-husband had called. She'd been expecting it for a while now, but had hoped she was wrong.

"She's got that campout in a couple of weeks. I'd told her I would go with her."

"But you've changed your mind." It wasn't a question.

"I hadn't realized it wasn't on our regular weekend. I've made other plans."

She gripped the receiver tightly. "This campout is very important to Allison. It's a father-daughter event. You've never done anything with her alone. She needs that, Nelson. She needs to know you care about her."

"Of course I care. What have you been telling her?"

He sounded outraged. If the situation wasn't so serious, she would have laughed. "I don't have to tell her anything. You're doing this all by yourself. You see the children every other weekend and no other time. You don't come to their school programs, you don't see them on holidays."

"I have a life. I have responsibilities."

She felt the first stirrings of temper. "You have two children. What is more important than that? They need more than visits every other weekend. They need to think you're a part of their lives and not some distant relative they see occasionally.''

"We've had this conversation before, Cindy. If you're upset about having to take care of the children, you should have thought about that before you insisted on getting pregnant. If you'll remember, I wanted to wait. I'm not getting into this with you again.''

He paused. She gritted her teeth. Now when they had these talks, she wondered what she'd been thinking when she'd married this man. With the hindsight of time, she realized she'd only seen Nelson's exterior package. She'd been blinded by the stable family and his career choice. She hadn't looked closely enough at the man behind the facade.

The mistake had been hers. She could live with that. What hurt the most was how her children had to suffer, too. It wasn't right. They deserved a father who loved them, not one who did what the court mandated and nothing else.

"Cindy, are you still there?'' he asked, his voice laced with irritation.

She sighed. "What's your point, Nelson?''

"I'm not going on the campout. I have plans with Hilari, and I'm not breaking them. I would like you to explain that to Allison, please.''

"Why should I do your dirty work for you?''

"If you don't want to tell her, then put her on the phone, and I'll do it myself.''

Cindy suspected Nelson wouldn't be kind to his daughter. "She's letting go of Shelby,'' she said softly. "After all this time, she goes hours, sometimes days without mentioning her. Doesn't that mean anything to you?''

"Who's Shelby?''

Cindy shook her head. Her ex-husband was hopeless. "I'll tell her myself," she said. "Goodbye, Nelson."

She hung up without waiting for his reply. She'd tried, but it had been too late for years. Nelson was right—he hadn't wanted children as much as she had. He'd wanted to wait. But she'd insisted. It was all part of her plan to be normal. It hadn't worked, of course, and she had a lot of regrets. But having children wasn't one of them. Her kids were the best part of her life. If she had a chance to do it all again, she would willingly marry Nelson, put up with him and his leaving simply because she couldn't imagine life without Allison and Jonathan.

She walked to the back door and called her daughter. The smiling child raced toward the house. Laughter lit up her eyes. Her children deserved better than Nelson. So she would lie for him. Make up a business meeting he'd tried hard to break. She wondered how long the lies would work. At some point in his life, Nelson was going to realize what he'd lost with his children. She liked to think she was a decent person, but chances were she was going to be right there telling him he only had himself to blame.

Mike left the jogging path and angled up toward the cul-de-sac. His breath came in pants and sweat dripped from him. He supposed he deserved it for running in the late afternoon. The temperature was only in the upper eighties, but the humidity was almost that high. He slowed to a walk and pulled off his T-shirt. He used the damp cloth to wipe his face.

As he walked in front of Cindy's house, he resisted the urge to glance over and see if she was home. He was doing his best to stay out of her way. The less contact they had, the better.

By the time he reached Grace's back door, his breathing had slowed to normal. He stepped into the cool kitchen and headed for the refrigerator. He'd left a half-gallon bottle of water on the top shelf. In the time he was running, the water had cooled some but wasn't really cold. He could down the whole thing without worrying about stomach cramps.

He tossed his T-shirt over one of the kitchen chairs and grabbed the bottle. Tilting his head back, he began to drink.

He was getting stronger every day. His workouts at the country-club gym were starting to pay off, although he was damn tired of his audience. Most of the men stayed away, but the number of women using the treadmills and other pieces of equipment had been constant.

He set the bottle on the counter and drew in a couple of breaths. Before he could pick it up again, the back door flew open and Allison raced toward him.

There were tears in her eyes and on her cheeks. Her face scrunched up in pain. Instinctively, he crouched and held out his arms. She barreled into him, crying as if her heart were broken.

"What's wrong?" he asked, running his hands down her back and legs, checking for an injury. "Did you fall down?"

"No," she said, clinging to him.

She buried her head in his shoulder. He could feel her hot breath and tears against his bare skin. "Are you hurt?"

"No..." This time the word was broken by a sob.

He shifted until he was kneeling on the floor and rocked her back and forth. Her crying continued, loud sobs punctuated by hiccuping breaths and shaking.

Finally, she raised her head and stared at him. Her green eyes were dark with tears. Her nose was red, her cheeks flushed. "I'm running away," she said. "I want you to drive me."

"Where do you want to go?"

She thought for a minute, then brushed her hand across her cheeks and sniffed. "Far away."

"Why?"

Fresh tears filled her eyes. "My daddy isn't going on the campout. I'm going to be the onliest girl there without a daddy."

Mike grimaced. Cindy had mentioned the campout a while ago, voicing her concerns that Nelson wouldn't bother to attend. Allison had also talked about the event. He knew it was important to her. For a moment, he thought about finding Nelson and explaining the facts of life to the man. Nelson couldn't continue to ignore his children. Then Mike figured Nelson wouldn't listen. Instead of talking, Mike decided he should just beat the hell out of him.

He had a feeling Cindy wouldn't approve of his actions. Besides, beating up Nelson would only make *him* feel good. Allison was the one who was hurting.

"Are you mad at your mother?" he asked.

She shook her head. "Mommy says she's coming with me in his place. I want Mommy to go, but it's not the same."

"I know, darling." He pulled her close and kissed the top of her head. "Running away is going to hurt your mother though, and she's not the one you're mad at. Have you thought of that?"

"No..." The sobs were back.

He held her as she cried. She smelled of grass and little girl. She felt so fragile in his arms, so easily bruised by the world and by her own father. He knew all about a parent hurting a kid. He'd lived it. If there was any justice, Nelson would hook up with someone as self-centered as himself.

"Your mother would be frightened if you ran away. She'd think that you didn't love her anymore. Do you want her to think that?"

"I love Mommy." The voice was muffled against his skin. He could feel the hot breaths of air. "But Daddy doesn't love me."

It was as if someone had jerked his heart out of his chest. He fought against the physical pain. Damn. He wasn't the right person to be having this conversation with Allison. He didn't know the first thing about raising kids. He was probably going to scar her for life, but he had to try to make her understand the truth.

"You are a wonderful girl," he said slowly. "You're bright and kind. You're good to your friends and very sweet. You also have the prettiest face I've ever seen. Your parents love you very much." He had his doubts about Nelson, but Allison didn't need to know that. "Grownups sometimes get so caught up in their own lives. Your father has forgotten how much fun it is to be with you. Until he remembers, he's going to do silly things, like canceling your campout. But just because he forgets, it doesn't mean he doesn't love you. It's not your fault. It's his."

She raised her gaze to his. He could see the confusion there. These were pretty complex thoughts for a seven-year-old. But even if she didn't understand everything he was saying, he wanted her to get the gist. Nelson was the jerk, not her.

"I like you very much," he said. "If I had a little girl of my own, I would want her to be just like you."

Her smile blossomed like a flower opening in sunlight. He touched the dimple in her cheek. He'd spoken the words to make her feel better, but at that moment, he knew they were true.

"I like you, too," she whispered.

The wound in his chest began to heal.

Fighting a sudden burst of emotion, he rose to his feet and held out his hand. "Your mom is probably worried about you. Let's head over there and tell her you're okay."

Allison came with him willingly. As he walked around the front of Cindy's house, he saw her in the garage, going through boxes. He sent Allison inside and continued down the driveway.

The three-car garage had a workbench running along the back. There were a few tools hanging from a Peg-Board. The minivan filled the space on the right. Several boxes marked Christmas Decorations stood against the left wall. Three bikes took the place of the second car. Next to them was the pile of boxes Cindy was going through. She'd pulled out sleeping bags and a lantern.

"What are you doing?" he asked.

She glanced up at him and grimaced. "Nelson punked out of the camping trip. Allison is heartbroken."

"I know. She came to my house. She wanted to run away and needed me to drive her."

Cindy paled. "Is she—"

"She's fine. I brought her home. We had a talk." He shifted his feet. "I don't know if I said the right thing or not, so you might want to talk to her." He hesitated, not sure how much he should tell her. "She knows it's not your fault."

"Oh, but it is. I married the jerk."

A headband held her hair off her face. A single strand drifted over her eyes and she brushed it away. Her expression was defeated. He wanted to comfort her, but somehow doing that had been easier with Allison. Maybe because his relationship with the child was less complicated.

She reached into the box and pulled out several flashlights. "This isn't the first time Nelson has done this to her. But it's never been with something this big. I thought—" She shook her head. "This is her first campout. I'd had such hopes for her. What is she going to remember when she looks back on this?" She drew in a deep breath. "It doesn't matter. I swear, that little girl is going to have the time of her life. I'm going to make sure of it. I've already arranged for Jonathan to stay with a friend."

"You're going in Nelson's place?"

She nodded. "They need some mothers to come along, anyway. I wasn't going to go because I didn't want to be in such close quarters with Nelson. Now that's not a problem. My only concern is that Allison is going to be the only girl there without an adult male along. Some of the girls don't have fathers, but they all have uncles or big brothers or something."

"We've already talked about this, Cindy. I'm happy to go."

She gave him a weary smile. "That's really nice but not necessary."

"I don't mind." He didn't. Allison was a sweet kid. He enjoyed her company. The idea of spending four days with Cindy was torture, but not the unpleasant kind. Besides, fifty or so little girls would be great chaperons.

"You're crazy."

"Maybe," he admitted. "I've never been around children. I just assumed I didn't like them, but that's not true. I like yours. I like the kids in the neighborhood." Selfishly, when Allison remembered her first campout, he wanted her to remember him. It was as close as he could come to belonging.

She tilted her head. "What do you know about camping?"

He grinned. "Everything. I used to be a marine."

"So if enemy forces attack the beach, you'll know just what to do?"

"Exactly." He folded his arms over his chest. "I'm great with camp food."

"Do you know how often little girls have to go to the bathroom in the night? They always wake up an adult. They aren't allowed to do anything by themselves. Everything is the buddy system. Are you prepared for that?"

"This isn't about me, it's about Allison. If I went, she would fit in with the other girls. She wouldn't be the only one without a guy. I might not be her father, but I'm a pretty good substitute."

Cindy blinked several times. It took him a moment to figure out she was fighting tears. "You've only known my children six weeks, but you're already a better father than Nelson ever was." She sniffed. "Thanks, Mike. I really appreciate your offer and I hope the campout isn't too horrible for you."

"It'll be fun."

She moved close to him. "Let's go tell Allison. She'll be thrilled."

Her gaze met his. He could see the tears darkening her irises to the color of emeralds. Her mouth trembled. He wanted to claim it with his own. Not because he wanted her—although he did—but to comfort her. Because he cared.

Caring scared him more than a psycho with a .45. It scared him more than dying.

Chapter Eleven

"Is everybody ready?" Cindy asked.

Six little girls looked at her and nodded earnestly. She raised her hands to cover her ears and yelled, "Go!"

Instantly, the loud, high-pitched scream of whistles filled the air. The seven-year-olds kept blowing until Cindy could feel the pounding start high in her temples. She forced herself to keep smiling. She'd learned a lot of tricks on camping trips with Jonathan and this was one of them.

"What are you doing?" Mike yelled over the sounds of the whistles.

She couldn't hear what he was saying, but she read his lips. "Getting it out of their systems. They have to wear their whistles at all times and blow them if there's an emergency. It's just too much temptation for most kids. This way—" The sound stopped. Cindy lowered her hands to her sides and glanced at the girls. They giggled together. After one or two short peeps, there was blissful silence.

"This way," she continued in a normal voice, "they've had their fun. Now they can ignore the whistles unless there's a problem."

He shook his head. "It's not like the marines."

"I'll bet."

She followed his gaze and saw about sixty little girls and their fathers milling through the camp. The kids were sleeping in platform tents. Most of the tents had yet to be erected. Fathers, some experienced campers, most not, argued with one another and their children over the best way to put up the tents.

The adults slept on the ground. Mike had already taken care of putting up their two small tents and Cindy was grateful. Camping wasn't her favorite activity, but she was willing to be here for Allison. Helping her daughter have a good time was all that mattered.

The crowd had no order, no leadership. Loud voices rose. Some of the girls were already crying. "You want to take over as drill sergeant?" she asked.

"Don't tempt me."

Cindy returned her attention to the six girls. Each small group had a woman assigned to them. It meant the fathers didn't have to deal with personal business such as supervising showers. Not that the girls were going to bathe very much over the next four days.

Most of the men were talking to one another and not their children. Cindy supposed they didn't know what was expected of them. There was going to be a general meeting in about a half hour, then dinner. At the meeting, the camp director, Mrs. Stewart, would explain the rules of the camp.

"We should probably get the cook fire started now," Cindy said. "That way the coals will be ready when the meeting is over."

"Coals?" He raised his eyebrows. "You guys really rough it, huh?"

"They are just little girls." She smiled. "Wait until you see dinner."

"Fast food?"

"No, prepared plates. I made one for you. Everything is cooked. We just heat it over the fire. Sort of like an open-air microwave."

"You're kidding?"

She leaned close. "Did you expect them to hunt for their meals? Maybe eat grubs and berries?"

His dark eyes crinkled at the corners as he smiled. "At least they'd learn something that way."

"Yeah, they'd learn they didn't like camping."

They exchanged a look of understanding and connection. Cindy felt the pull clear to her belly. She tried to resist it as much as she could. There was no reason for them to impress anyone here with their supposed relationship. They could drop the act and go back to being friends. But she found she didn't want to. She liked Mike putting his arm around her and holding her close. She liked the way he looked at her as if he thought she was pretty. She liked pretending it was real.

A very dangerous line of thought, she told herself.

Before she could say or do something, she was rescued by a pretty woman holding a can of bug repellent.

"Hi, Cindy. I don't know if you remember me. I'm Pam," the woman said. Her thick brown hair was cut short. Green eyes danced with humor.

"Of course I do." Cindy grinned. "You were at the last campout I came on. It was all boys then."

Pam nodded. "Girls should be a lot easier. At least we won't have that snake-catching contest."

Both women shuddered.

"Is your husband with you?" Cindy asked.

Pam laughed. "Are you kidding? Pass up an opportunity to sleep in dirt and fight with fire ants? He wouldn't miss it." She glanced at Mike. "And this is . . . ?"

"Oh, I'm sorry. Mike Blackburne, this is Pam East. Mike is a friend of the family. He's my daughter's substitute father for the weekend."

They shook hands. "Nice of you to come along," Pam said.

"I wanted to," Mike told her.

Pam held up the can of spray. "I'm responsible for insect dieting. If you haven't sprayed up, you need to. The girls, too. Any of you need an extra dose?"

"No, thanks. We coated the girls before we let them out of the car."

"See you," Pam said and walked to the next group of children.

Cindy watched her go. "It's not fair," she said when the other woman was out of earshot.

"What isn't fair?"

"Pam and Steve. They're a great couple. I met them the last time I came camping. They accompany several campouts each summer, giving up their vacation time." She looked at Mike and grimaced. "They don't have any kids of their own. They've been trying for years, but nothing. They're hoping for a private adoption. Who knows how long that's going to take." She drew in a deep breath. "Last I heard, they'd about given up. It's a shame. There are parents like Nelson who don't even care about their kids, then there are people like Pam and Steve who can't have them."

"You mean, they come on the campouts just because they want to help?"

He sounded so startled, she laughed. "Yes, Mike. Some people like children."

"I don't dislike them. I'm just surprised."

"That there are good people in the world?"

"Maybe. I don't see a lot of them in my line of work."

She wanted to go to him and hold him. Before she could give in to the impulse, a call came for the camp meeting. Cindy and Mike collected the girls and walked slowly toward the open meeting area.

A small platform had been built at one end. Everyone settled on the ground. Cindy sat down cross-legged and realized her butt was too old to be comfortable without a real chair. Mike struggled to find a comfortable position. If the look on his face was anything to go by, the healing muscles in his thigh weren't happy about being stretched out. Allison shimmied between them and plopped onto the ground.

She grinned. "I like camping."

Cindy brushed Allison's bangs out of her face. "You haven't actually done any yet."

"But I still like it."

"I'm glad." She kissed her daughter's forehead.

The camp director, Mrs. Stewart, stepped up onto the platform. She welcomed everyone to the father-daughter camp, then proceeded to read from a list of rules. Cindy knew most of them by heart. The most important one was the buddy system. No child was to go off by herself. Anywhere. Not even to the rest room. The talk went on.

Cindy glanced around the open area. It had been cleared of brush and trees. There were patches of grass, but by late July, hundreds of campers' feet had worn most of it away. Tall trees ringed the camp. In another half hour or so they would provide shade from the sun. Cindy wiped her forehead. It wasn't too bad, only in the eighties. For a Houston summer, that was practically chilly. The humidity was low, too, which was a pleasant change.

"The beach is off-limits tonight," Mrs. Stewart was saying. "The alligators are out."

"Alligators?" Mike asked quietly.

"Sure. They're in the river." She smiled. "This is swampland, what did you expect?"

"You camp near alligators?"

"It's a great punishment if the kids get out of hand. We just hold them by their ankles and dangle them over the water." She could feel a smile tugging at the corners of her mouth, but she kept her face serious.

Allison looked at her. "Really?" she asked, her eyes big.

Cindy nodded.

"I'll be good, Mommy."

"I know you will."

"So that's how it is," Mike said and winked.

It was a silly meaningless gesture that made her tingle all the way to her toes.

When the meeting was over, Allison and her friends scrambled to their feet. The parents rose more slowly. Mike stood up and held out his hand. Cindy placed her fingers against his and allowed him to pull her up. She brushed off her shorts, then grimaced.

"We forgot to start the fire for dinner. The girls are going to be hungry and cranky."

"No problem," he said. "I saw starter cans in with the cooking supplies."

When they got back to their section of the camp, three men had collected around the fire pit. They were arguing over the best way to start the fire. One little girl stood nearby, her expression mutinous.

"But, Daddy, we *can't* use starter fluid. It's against the rules."

"Do you want to follow the rules, or do you want to eat?" the man asked, obviously annoyed.

"Try these," Mike said, handing him a starter can. He then showed the man how to stuff newspaper into the can, followed by charcoal briquettes. Mike lit the paper on fire. After a few minutes, he used tongs to pull away the can.

Allison laughed and clapped her hands together. "They're already red."

Cindy smiled. "I'm impressed, Blackburne."

The children got out their prepared dinners and set them on the grill. One girl had a whole yam. Mike looked at it, then at her. "Honey, this isn't going to cook until morning."

"Mommy said it would be good for me. Lots of vitamins. I don't have anything else." Her voice trembled.

Allison spoke up. "I'll share my dinner," she said. "I have lots."

The two girls sat next to each other on a log. Mike stepped around it and moved next to Cindy. "Don't ever question your abilities as a parent."

She stared at her youngest, then shook her head. "I'd like to take credit for that, but I think it's just her. She's a sweet kid."

Slowly, all the meals were heated and everyone sat down to eat. Several of the men jockeyed for position, as if one's status at a campout was as important as the hierarchy in a boardroom. A few fathers ignored the posturing and settled beside their daughters, clearly enjoying the time with them.

Mike stayed near Allison and her new friend. He made sure they had enough to drink, then brought Cindy her meal. When everyone had eaten and the plates had been cleared away, he and Steve started the marshmallow detail so everyone could have S'mores.

Mrs. Stewart came by and began singing camp songs.

"Something tells me this isn't how the marines do it," Cindy said, leaning close to Mike. He was helping a girl fit a marshmallow over the end of a green stick. When the sticky treat caught fire, he blew it out and gently directed her to hold it over some smoldering coals.

"We didn't roast a lot of marshmallows," he admitted, leaning back against the log. "But we did sit around fires at night."

"Telling lies about women?"

"Mostly."

It was nearly dark, but she saw the flash of white teeth as he smiled. "What were your lies?"

"That I knew any woman. I was very skinny when I was eighteen."

She almost mentioned the fact that he'd definitely filled out some since then, but managed to hold back the words. Mike had enough trouble with women falling all over him without her starting to do it, too.

When all the girls had their fill of dessert, he roasted a couple of marshmallows for her. The off-key singing continued. Songs about stars and animals and old folk tunes. The children laughed when they didn't know the words, or made up new ones. Cindy liked the closeness of the moment, and the feel of Mike next to her. When he put his arm around her, she leaned against his shoulder.

"I like Pam," he said.

Cindy glanced through the smoldering fire and saw Pam and Steve sitting across from them. They were feed-

ing each other marshmallows and smiling in that special
way lovers do.

"Why?" she asked.

"She barely noticed I was alive."

Cindy laughed. "You're right. She wasn't the least bit
impressed by you." Her laughter faded as she studied the
couple. "They're so happy together. I envy them. They
have everything I always wanted."

"I'm tired, Mommy," Allison said and crawled into her
lap. The child shifted so she was half on Mike, as well,
then rested her head on his chest.

Mike touched her daughter's hair. "You have what they
want," he said quietly.

He was right, Cindy thought. Life wasn't fair. But
sometimes, like now, it was very close to perfect.

"Cindy, wake up."

Someone was shaking her arm. She pulled the sleeping
bag up over her head. "Go away."

"I'm going to stay right here until you wake up."

That voice. She recognized it. What was Mike doing in
her bedroom? What was she doing sleeping on the
ground?

"Oh, we're camping," she muttered and raised her
head. "What do you want?" She squinted. "It's still
dark. Go away. Do you know how many times I had to
take little girls to the bathroom last night? Fifty-seven. Or
was it twenty? I can't remember. I just know I barely got
any sleep."

"You have to get up."

She pushed the hair from her eyes. "You're disgust-
ing," she said, glaring at his smiling face. "No one should
look that good in the morning. I feel as puffy and attractive as a blowfish. Go away."

Mike glanced over his shoulder, then reached into her sleeping bag and grabbed her arms. Before she could protest, he pulled her out and set her on the covers. "You've got three minutes to get dressed, Cindy. If you're not ready, you're coming with us the way you are."

"Who is us and where are we going?"

"It's a surprise."

"I hate surprises," she muttered, but he was already gone.

At that moment, she happened to glance down at herself. She bit back a moan. She'd known the girls would come to her to escort them to the rest rooms in the night so she'd gone to bed wearing shorts under her nightshirt. However, in her fitful sleep, it had twisted off one shoulder, exposing plenty of flesh. Mike hadn't even noticed. So much for dazzling the man with her feminine charms. She probably looked so old and haggard, he couldn't register anything else.

She drew the tent flaps together and quickly put on a bra and shirt. After spraying again with bug repellent, she slipped on socks and shoes, grabbed a flashlight, then made a mad dash for the rest room. A quick combing restored her hair to almost normal. She splashed water on her face and brushed her teeth. She was back at her tent in less than five minutes.

The western horizon was still dark, but dawn was breaking to the east. Mike was waiting for her with Allison and two of the little girl's friends.

"Where are we going?" Cindy asked again.

Mike put a finger to his lips and started walking away from the camp.

Cindy and the girls followed silently. After about fifteen minutes, they came to a clearing. A small house belonging to the park ranger stood at one end. There was a fenced garden and green grass. Mike paused by the edge of the lawn.

As if their presence had triggered a prearranged signal, a doe and two fawns stepped out of the bushes. The girls gasped.

The creatures moved with long-legged grace. Their smooth coats were almost gray in the predawn light. The back door of the house opened and the park ranger put out a large dish of food.

"They're beautiful," Allison breathed. Her friends agreed.

The silence stretched on as the animals ate. The babies finished first, then began a game of tag in the clearing. They chased each other, jumping playfully over imaginary barriers.

The girls stared raptly. Cindy felt her throat tighten with emotion as Allison shyly took hold of Mike's hand. He squeezed her fingers and smiled down at her. Allison smiled back.

Cindy knew her daughter would remember this moment forever. She would share it with her children, telling them about the first time she'd watched fawns frolic in the early morning.

Cindy knew she would remember this moment, too. It marked the exact second her daughter fell in love with Mike. Allison had handed over her heart with a child's trust that the affection would be returned. Cindy wondered if her own heart was far behind.

Mike glanced at her. "What do you think?" he asked softly.

"They're wonderful," she said, motioning to the fawns. The mother had finished eating but seemed content to let her children play.

Mike knelt in the damp grass and pointed out the different markings on the fawns. The girls listened intently. Again she marveled at how much better Mike was with the children than Nelson had ever been. Maybe some fathers were born, not made. She wondered what Mike would be like with his own children.

The thought was as tempting as chocolate to someone on a diet. She didn't want to dwell on it, but once it was in her mind, she couldn't get rid of it.

She reminded herself that men like Mike didn't stay. But that didn't erase her desire to see him holding a baby of his own. Her baby.

"When you have enough beads to fit around your wrist, add a couple extra so the bracelet will dangle," Cindy said. "We don't want it so tight, it cuts off your circulation."

Several of the girls looked up at her and giggled. Mike smiled as he patrolled the tables, making sure everyone concentrated on her craft. "Stay two arm's-lengths apart," he cautioned, trying to avoid the inevitable stabbing with the dull needles used to string the beads.

"Bet they didn't do much of this in the marines," Cindy whispered as he circled behind her.

"You're right." He gave her short ponytail a playful tug, then returned his attention to the girls.

Most of the fathers were over with the knot-tying group. He was willing to admit it was more macho to tie knots than make bead bracelets, but he wasn't on the trip to affirm his masculinity. He was here to be with Allison and this was the craft she'd chosen.

"My cord's got a kink in it," one of the little girls wailed.

Mike was instantly at her side. He slipped off a couple of beads, smoothed the cord until it was straight, then handed it to the now-smiling child. "Better than new," he said.

Pam walked over to him and placed her hands on her hips. "You're very good at this. Cindy has been telling us you don't have kids, but I'm starting to wonder."

"I've spent the summer practicing," he said. "Allison and her brother live right next door."

"You've learned well." Pam glanced from him to Cindy. "Maybe you should think of having a few of your own."

"No way." He raised his hands in a gesture of surrender. "I move around a lot."

Her smile faded and her green eyes darkened with sadness. "It's a waste, if you ask me."

Before they could continue the conversation, Pam stepped away to help another child. Mike watched her go. As he'd told Cindy, he liked Pam; she didn't treat him any differently than she treated any of the other men. She knew he was a single guy, a bodyguard, and she couldn't care less. It was refreshing. Cindy had teased him about being disappointed not to add one more member to his fan club, but in truth he was relieved. There was only one woman he wanted fawning on him and that was Cindy.

His gaze drifted over to his next-door neighbor and ersatz girlfriend. Cindy was bending over the table helping one of the girls. Her shorts pulled tight around her rear and he wished he were standing behind her so he could admire the view.

Down, boy, he told himself silently. This wasn't the time or the place. Although she was awfully tempting with her sunburned nose and no makeup. She wasn't the glamorous type he usually dated. She was genuine and caring.

She didn't play games and when she gave her heart, it was forever. He wished he were a different kind of man. Someone who would be able to give her what she needed and deserved.

Cindy finished with the girl and strolled over to him. "How's it going? You want to make some jewelry for Grace?"

"I think she'll be buying all she needs in Hong Kong."

"But a necklace or bracelet from you would be very special."

He made a fist and pretended to clip her jaw. He brushed against her soft skin. Longing swept through him. "You think you're very funny."

"I don't just think it, I know it for a fact." She smiled, then pointed at Pam. "I saw you two talking."

"I'm still surprised that she and Steve come on these trips, and they don't have any kids of their own."

"Some people believe in giving something back."

Interesting concept, he thought. What did he ever give back?

Before he could answer that question, a messenger van pulled up to the edge of camp. A young man stepped out. "I'm looking for Steve and Pam East," he said loudly.

Pam heard him. She turned and paled. Mike understood her concern. The envelope in the messenger's hand looked ominous.

"I wonder what's wrong," Cindy said. Most of the girls stopped what they were doing and watched.

Steve raced over to his wife and put his arm around her. Together they approached the messenger. The man handed them the envelope. The normally noisy camp grew silent; even the insects seemed to have stopped buzzing. Cindy clutched Mike's arm.

"I hope nobody died," she whispered.

Steve and Pam read the message. Pam threw herself into her husband's arms and started to cry. Cindy jogged toward her. Mike followed. Then he realized the couple wasn't sad. They were laughing. Steve swung his wife around.

Pam glanced up at Cindy. "We're going to have a baby. A birth mother has chosen us. We met with her last week, and we almost decided not to come on the campout so we could wait by the phone for her answer, but she was taking her school exams and said she wouldn't decide until Monday. I guess she changed her mind." She smiled through her tears. "Next to falling in love with Steve, this is the most wonderful thing that has ever happened to me."

Cindy hugged her friend. The other women in the camp approached and embraced as the men shook hands.

"We're going to have to leave right away," Pam said, wiping her face. "The baby is due in less than two weeks. There are a million things to prepare. A baby."

Her happiness was so bright it nearly blinded him. As she moved toward her tent to collect her belongings, she paused in front of Mike.

"Are you sure this is what you want?" she asked.

He didn't have an answer so he hugged her.

"I'm so happy," she said. Steve came over and the two men shook hands.

Mike watched as everyone helped them pack. In less than fifteen minutes, the couple was heading back to Houston. He stood on the edge of the crowd, strangely detached from their joy. He was happy Pam and Steve were finally going to have their child, but he didn't understand why they'd wanted one so much in the first place. At times, he didn't feel completely human. It was as if some of his emotions had atrophied from disuse.

Cindy picked up Allison and held her close. Mother and daughter clung to each other, their love visible to him. The pain in his chest told him that his heart was working. He still felt the pain of being on the outside, looking in.

"I want to call Daddy and tell him I had a good time," Allison said as Cindy pulled into the driveway. The girl had unfastened her seat belt and had the side door open before Cindy had set the parking brake.

"He might not be home," Cindy called after her. "And you can't get inside until I unlock the door."

Allison danced impatiently. Cindy rolled her eyes at Mike. "I think her first campout was a success."

"Seems that way."

Cindy wondered what was bothering him. He'd been quiet for a couple of days now. The nearest she could pinpoint it, he'd started acting withdrawn right after Pam and Steve had left. She wasn't sure why that would have upset him.

She heard a call from across the greenbelt. Jonathan burst out of his friend's house and ran toward home.

"You guys are finally back," he yelled.

Cindy gave her keys to an impatient Allison, then turned to greet her son. He hugged her tight then frowned. "Next time, I want to go camping with you guys. You had all the fun, and I was just stuck here with nothing to do."

"Interesting. I could have sworn Brett's mother said you guys were going to Astro World, to the movies and ice skating. Didn't you do any of that?"

"Sure, but it wasn't camping with Mike." He turned to the man. "How was it? Were the girls all real dumb?"

Mike pulled camping gear out of the rear of the mini-van. "We had fun."

"I want to go on a camping trip, too," Jonathan said. "Mike, will you take me?"

Mike straightened, a sleeping bag under each arm. He drew his eyebrows together, obviously surprised. "You want to go camping with me?"

"Sure. It would be great. Just us guys. You know, roughing it."

"We'll talk about this later," Cindy said, rescuing Mike. The poor man didn't know what to say. "Go inside and see if your sister has gotten hold of her father. You can talk to him, too."

When Jonathan slammed the back door shut behind him, she turned to Mike. "Sorry about that. I didn't know he was going to put you on the spot. There's really no time between now and when school starts, and it's unlikely you'll be coming back later in the fall. I'll explain it to him."

"I wouldn't mind going. Maybe around Thanksgiving."

That sounded suspiciously like a long-term commitment. "Why would you want to?"

"I like Jonathan."

"I know, but—" She didn't know how to explain it without sounding like a fool. "Thanks."

She grabbed a cooler and headed for the house. Inside her stomach she felt a flicker of hope. She doused it with a large dose of reality. Agreeing to go camping with a nine-year-old boy wasn't the same as making an emotional commitment to her. This was all temporary. When he was healed and the time was up, Mike would be moving on. Occasional visits wouldn't be enough for her.

She was still looking for a sure thing.

Chapter Twelve

Cindy closed the door to Jonathan's room and sighed. It had taken the better part of an hour to get them both calm enough to sleep. Allison had to be exhausted from the camping trip and, according to Brett's mother, Jonathan and Brett had been staying up late playing video games, so getting them to bed shouldn't have been a problem. But nothing was as it was supposed to be with children. There were always surprises.

Like Jonathan wanting to go camping with Mike. She probably shouldn't be all that shocked. Her son liked and respected Mike. It made sense he would want to spend time with the man. It wasn't as if Nelson ever did anything with the children aside from taking them every other weekend.

She walked along the hallway, then down the stairs and into the kitchen.

"They're finally asleep," she said. "I know they were exhausted, but they kept fighting it." Mike had already started the dishwasher and was finishing up with the pots. "You didn't have to do that," she said.

"You didn't have to invite me to stay for dinner," he answered easily. "I get tired of frozen meals."

"You could cook something yourself."

He glanced at her over his shoulder and grinned. "It's easier to wash your dishes."

She'd thought Mike would have had enough of her and children for one weekend, but when she'd invited him to stay and eat with them, he'd accepted. Jonathan had wanted to hear every detail of the camping trip and Allison had been in heaven, at last having something to hold over her older brother. Mike had kept both children entertained, reenacting the events of the campout.

She'd taken the opportunity to wash away the dust and grime. There had been showers at the campsite, but none she wanted to use. It was wonderful to finally have clean hair again. Mike had also showered and shaved, although if she were honest with herself, she would have to admit that she missed the stubble. It gave him a dark and dangerous look. As if he were a renegade, or an outlaw of some kind. As if his career wasn't romantic enough already.

"What are you smiling at?" he asked, picking up a dishcloth and drying the largest pot.

"Nothing. I'm just happy to be home with running water and electricity."

"That campground is hardly roughing it."

"It's wild enough for the likes of me. I've never seen the appeal of living with creepy-crawly things or sleeping in the dirt."

"It's getting back to nature."

"This from a man who lives in the city."

He winked. "Can't make a living from a tent."

"Probably not."

The sun had barely set in the western sky. There were still hints of pink in the clouds. Outside, fireflies danced through the greenbelt. Other invisible creatures had taken up their nightly chorus. She and Mike were standing in her kitchen. He was drying pots, for heaven's sake, and her kids were sleeping upstairs. It wasn't a magical moment. And yet she felt very strange inside. Her stomach was filled with nervous fluttering. Her arms and legs felt both heavy and light. Her skin tingled.

Maybe it was because Mike's dark gaze never left hers. Maybe it was because they'd just spent four days together and neither of them seemed to want the time to be over. Maybe it was because she could remember what it felt like to be in his arms and right now there was nothing she wanted more.

She was barefoot. After her shower, she hadn't bothered putting on makeup. Her hair was straight, her clothing a simple T-shirt and shorts. Yet the way Mike was looking at her, she could have been dressed in black silk and pearls. She was drawn to him, drawn to the man who had taken the time to make her children feel special and herself feel desired. Except that he would leave her, he was everything she'd ever wanted.

Before she could step closer to him and perhaps make an incredible fool of herself, a car turned into the driveway. She glanced out the kitchen window and frowned. The red convertible looked familiar.

"That's Nelson's car. What's he doing here?"

Mike shrugged and went back to drying the pots. She started toward the back door, but before she got there, it flew open. Her ex-husband stomped inside.

He glanced from her to Mike, then frowned. "What the hell is going on here?"

His rudeness annoyed her almost as much as his question. "That's what I'd like to know," she said, marching past him and closing the door. She glared at him. "This is my house, Nelson. I bought you out. The deed is in *my* name. You no longer have the right to do as you please here. If you want to come inside, you knock."

"I told you to keep the door locked," Mike said.

"I should have listened."

Nelson stared at Mike. His gaze narrowed. "So you're the bodyguard."

Mike put down the pot he'd been drying and smiled. "You're the ex-husband."

The men were about the same height, with the same coloring. But there the similarity ended. Mike was lean and dangerous, trained to kill. Nelson sold insurance and had never done anything about the extra twenty pounds he'd gained.

Nelson turned back to her. "You had no right to take this paramilitary type camping with my daughter. Don't do it again."

"Are you crazy? You're telling me who can and can't see Allison? Is that right?"

"Yes. She's my daughter."

"Only when it's convenient for you. Mike did me a favor by coming with me. Allison was crushed when you backed out of the camping trip. She was in tears. Mike stepped in and made her feel better. He did your job for you."

She moved closer and stuck out her index finger. "While we're on the subject, don't you ever tell me who I can and can't see."

"I'll do what I damn well please," her ex-husband said, his brown eyes bright with anger. "You're their mother. You have to set an example."

His temper didn't frighten her. She was just as furious. "And you don't?" She didn't give him a chance to answer. "You're the one who dumped me, then lived with a woman before marrying her. Now you've dumped wife number two for Hilari. Yet you come in here and want to judge me? I'm a damn good mother to those children. It doesn't have anything to do with whom I do or don't see, it's about something else. Something you can't understand. It's about caring for them. It's about being with them when they need me. They count on me, Nelson. They know you only care when it's your weekend. But I'm *always* there for them."

"You've turned my children against me."

"No. You did that yourself."

"I won't let you live with this guy."

She didn't bother reminding him that Mike didn't live with her. That wasn't the point. "You don't have any say here. I'll do what I want."

Nelson flushed with anger. "You'd better listen to me."

"Or you'll what? Sue me for custody?" She smiled. "I don't think so. You couldn't be bothered."

Nelson took a step toward her. Cindy was startled by the physical threat, but she didn't budge. In the back of her mind, she wondered if Nelson was trying to act macho because Mike was here. That made her dislike her ex-husband even more.

"I wouldn't try that if I were you," Mike said softly.

Sometime while she and Nelson had been arguing, he'd put the dish towel and pot down and had approached. He stood balanced on the balls of his feet. Like a wildcat ready to pounce, he was pure coiled strength.

"On second thought, do it," Mike said, his voice still quiet. "Raise your hand to her, buddy, but make it good the first time because when I'm done with you, you'll never threaten a woman again."

Nelson drew himself up to his full height. "I've never hit a woman in my life. Is this what you've been doing, Cindy? Telling lies about me?"

"You've never hit any of us," she said. "I didn't tell anyone you had. That's not your style, Nelson. You prefer to walk out on your family."

The muscles in his jaw tightened. "Call off your trained attack dog so we can talk about this civilly."

"There's nothing to talk about," Mike said. "You're not married to Cindy anymore. You have no rights here."

"And you do?" Nelson asked.

"No. Cindy's in charge." Mike turned his gaze on her. "You want me to beat him up for you?"

Cindy held Mike's gaze. He wasn't angry. His offer came from a desire to protect her. There was a part of her that wanted to see Nelson broken and whimpering. He'd been pretty cruel when he'd left, making her feel as if the failure of the marriage was all her fault. For a long time, she'd thought she was too old and too unattractive to be of interest to any man. Mike had helped change that.

But punishing Nelson wouldn't accomplish anything. Still, she waited until a bead of sweat formed on her ex-husband's upper lip before slowly shaking her head no.

"No matter what I think of him personally, he's still the father of my children. It's better if we all behave like adults."

Nelson exhaled audibly, then reached for the door handle. "I'm outta here," he muttered. "You guys are crazy."

"You have the children next weekend," Cindy reminded him as he ran for his car. "Be sure to be nice to them."

She closed the door and leaned against it.

Mike came up behind her. "You mad at me?"

She smiled. "No one has ever defended my honor before. I'm not mad. I'm a little ashamed of myself, though. I kept picturing Nelson beat up and writhing on the floor. It was a lovely image."

"Guys like him need a little humbling every now and then." He returned to the kitchen and continued drying the pots.

She straightened and walked to the counter separating the kitchen from the family room. "He seemed so stable once. So normal. What a mistake to have married him," she mused aloud.

"Obviously. The guy's a fool."

"And a jerk."

"A wimp." He tossed her the towel. "Finish drying. It's my turn to pick the video we're watching." With that, he walked to the built-in bookcases on both sides of the TV and began scanning the titles.

Cindy stared at him. She'd already made one big mistake in her life by marrying Nelson. She didn't want to make another. Which, of course, meant her not getting involved with Mike.

Or was the mistake letting him go?

Mike had strung a hammock between the two pecan trees in Grace's backyard. He lay stretched out in the shade provided by the leafy trees. A paperback spy thriller was open on his chest, but he didn't feel like reading. It was enough just to relax, sip his beer and think about nothing. He could get used to this kind of life.

The neighborhood was quiet. Cindy's kids had left for their swim-team practice a couple of hours ago. He didn't know where the other neighborhood children were. It seemed like the perfect time to take a nap.

He closed his eyes. Immediately, he pictured Cindy. Her long curvy legs. The thrust of her breasts. The way she'd tasted and felt next to him. Her mouth had been—

The ringing of the phone cut through his thoughts. He reached for the cordless and pushed the on button.

"Yeah," he said into the receiver.

"Mr. Blackburne, this is Alicia from your answering service. You've had a call."

He took the information, then punched off the off button. A call. The world was knocking on his door again. He flexed his leg. It had been two months. It was already August. He was about as close to fit as he was going to be. In another couple of weeks, he would be at a hundred percent. There was no reason not to return to work.

But it was several minutes before he picked up the phone again and punched in the numbers. Even as it rang somewhere in Washington, he thought about hanging up. But he didn't.

"Hello?"

"This is Mike Blackburne. Mr. Anthony called me about a job."

"Ah, yes, you're the bodyguard. Thank you for calling so promptly, Mr. Blackburne. You come very highly recommended. Let me tell you a little about our problem."

Fifteen minutes later, Mike stretched out on the hammock and wondered if he'd made the right decision. The fact that he was even bothering to question it told him how far gone he was. He should be itching to get back to work. Usually, two weeks away from the game was all he could stand. It had been two months.

He tried to remember the thrill of the chase, the excitement of pitting his skills against those of the enemy. Suddenly, he felt nothing but tired and old. He didn't want to go.

The job started in three weeks. What was he going to tell Cindy? He grimaced. Would she even miss him? She'd known from the start that his visit was temporary. They'd both agreed they couldn't be more wrong for each other. So it shouldn't matter that he was finally moving on. Yet it did matter. He wondered how he was going to get through the day without her.

The gate latch clicked and Jonathan stepped into the backyard. "Hey, Mike," he called. "You wanna play ball?"

"Sure," Mike answered, pushing into a sitting position.

Jonathan's hair was shaggy, his body tanned from his hours in the sun. He looked like a typical kid. Mike was going to miss both him and Allison.

"How was swim practice?" he asked.

"Okay, I guess. We don't have any more meets or anything. It's almost time for school to start."

"Already?"

"Yeah. We get out at the beginning of June and go back in August. I wish we never had to go back." Jonathan's smile faded. "Are we going camping over Thanksgiving?"

It still surprised him that Jonathan wanted to. Cindy had tried to explain it to him several times. He could believe that the kids liked him—after all, he liked them, too. But the concept of making personal plans for the future was foreign.

"I don't know," Mike said truthfully. "I've got a new job, and I don't know how long I'll be on it."

Jonathan stared at him. His brown eyes widened. "What do you mean? Are you leaving?"

"I don't really live here," he said, motioning to the house. "Grace does. You knew I was just staying here for the summer."

"Yeah, but—" Jonathan turned away and his shoulders slumped. "I thought it was different."

"How?"

The boy didn't answer.

When the silence grew awkward, Mike cleared his throat. "Listen, I'll come back. Grace is here and she's my sister. I'll visit."

"You never visited before. I thought you liked us."

"I do."

"Then how can you leave?"

He stared at Jonathan's slender back. The kid was only nine. How could any of this make sense? "I've got a job. When it's done, I'll come back. I promise."

"But you'll leave a-again."

It took Mike a minute to figure out the break in Jonathan's voice meant he was crying. He didn't know what to do. Before he could offer comfort, the boy started walking away.

When he reached the gate, he pulled it open and stepped through onto the driveway. He glanced back at Mike. Tears filled his eyes and trickled down his cheeks. He brushed them away impatiently. "You're leaving," he repeated. "Just like my dad."

As the boy walked away, Mike realized Jonathan had already learned his mother's lesson. Men leave.

* * *

The two kids scrambled out of the car and dashed across the greenbelt. "Be sure to say thank-you for being invited," Cindy called after them.

She got a vague wave in response. Brett had invited Jonathan to a movie and early dinner and had agreed to let Allison tag along. After a day spent shopping for school clothes, the silence was going to be a welcome relief.

She opened the back of the minivan and pulled out several bags. The kids had sprouted during the summer and they needed almost everything new. She'd been saving Nelson's child support for the last three months and had used up most of it in a single shopping trip. The price of the shoes alone had nearly sent her into cardiac arrest.

She clutched the bags in one hand and fumbled with her keys with the other. After opening the back door, she tossed the bags on the sofa, then walked into the kitchen to pour herself a glass of iced tea. She was taking a sip when she saw someone prowling in her backyard.

Her first instinct was to scream for Mike, but she didn't know if he was even home. She hadn't seen much of him in the last couple of days. Her second thought was to dial 911. She'd just reached for the phone when the man moved closer to the family room windows.

The receiver fell to the floor. A sharp pain cut through her midsection. She fought against the need to double over. Her breathing was labored, her mouth dry. Then the sensations passed and she was left with a giant hole where her heart used to be.

The prowler wasn't a stranger. It was Mike. She hadn't recognized him because he'd cut his hair. Once again, the short, military style exposed his ears and the back of his neck. She knew what that meant . . . he was leaving.

She replaced the receiver then walked to the back door and opened it. "You want some tea?" she asked, trying to sound calm.

He glanced at her. "Sure." He came inside and pointed to the windows. "I was checking your security. You've got one or two broken latches. I'll fix them. Have you thought about getting an alarm put in?"

"No." She could barely get the word out.

After pouring his tea, she added the correct amount of sugar. He took the glass, then glanced at the packages on the sofa. "You've been busy."

"School starts in two weeks. The kids needed new clothes. I got some things, too. It looks like we'll all be back to work. Including you," she said as nonchalantly as she could.

He leaned against the counter. "Jonathan told you."

"No, I figured it out all by myself."

"How?"

"The haircut."

"Oh." He reached up and touched his bare neck. "I guess it doesn't exactly fit in around here."

The hole in her chest wasn't getting any smaller and she was finding it difficult to keep breathing. "You told Jonathan?"

"A couple of days ago. He was asking me about the camping trip. I said I would come back, but I can't know exactly when." His eyes darkened. "I mean to keep my word, Cindy. Maybe you could tell him that."

"I will. You're not Nelson. You'll take him camping. But Jonathan won't believe you until you actually show up. He's been disappointed too many times by his dad."

"I'm sorry for that."

"It's not your fault."

She couldn't believe they were having this very normal, very rational conversation when all she wanted to do was scream at him. How could he just walk out of her life? It wasn't supposed to happen this way. She wasn't supposed to care.

She set her drink on the center island and forced herself to smile. "When do you leave?"

"The job starts in three weeks. I'll need a few days to get my things in order. I've got to pick up my business suits from the dry cleaners in L.A. I probably have a few papers to go through. That sort of thing. I was planning on leaving a week from Friday."

She didn't want to ask but she couldn't help herself. "Were you going to tell me or were you just going to disappear?" She hated that her voice was shaking.

"Cindy." He put his drink down and moved close to her. "I was going to say something today. That's why I was looking at the house. I want things to be okay after I'm gone."

"I've managed to survive all these years without you. I think I'll continue to make it."

"That's not what I meant."

Emotions swirled around her, through her. She didn't understand them. Mike wasn't breaking the rules, she was. She'd known from the first minute they'd met that he was leaving. He'd never once tried to convince her otherwise. So what was her problem? Why did she want to break down and cry? Why did she want him to hold her and promise to never go away? Nothing made sense.

It wasn't fair.

He touched her chin, forcing her to look at him. The handsome lines of his face made her heart ache. He'd been so good to her and to her kids. He'd made her remember what it was like to be a woman, and to be alive. She was going to miss that.

"Indulge me," he murmured. "Let me pretend you'll miss me and not do well without me. And get those damn window locks fixed."

She smiled. "You can do it yourself if you want."

"Thanks." His fingers stroked her cheek. For a minute, she thought he was going to kiss her, but he didn't.

"I'll miss you," he said. "You've been a good friend to me. You helped me fit in here."

"No problem," she said airily as she moved away from him. She clutched the tea glass as if it were a lifeline. "I was just doing Grace a favor." She sounded fine. It was good that he didn't know how much that cost her.

"You didn't have to pretend to be involved with me. Is that going to be okay?"

"What do you mean?"

He shrugged. "I don't want people thinking you got dumped. Why don't you tell everyone I turned out to be a jerk."

"I'll be fine, Mike. People will think what they like and there's nothing we can do about it. Beth knows the truth. She'll tell the rest of our friends. No one else matters."

They stared at each other. It was as if they both had so much to say, but it was all too dangerous. She wasn't going to ask him to stay and he wasn't going to offer. It was better this way. The leaving would be swift and painful, like a burn. In time, she would heal and only she would be able to see the scar.

Chapter Thirteen

"Mike's leaving," Cindy said, slouching in her chair at the kitchen table.

"When?" Beth asked.

"In a week and a half." She resisted the urge to sigh. She was acting like a melodramatic teenager. The only problem was she didn't know how to stop.

"You seem surprised. His visit here has always been temporary."

"I know that," Cindy snapped. "That doesn't mean I have to like it."

Beth stared at her wide-eyed, then straightened in her chair and took a sip of tea. "I guess you told me," she said softly.

Cindy leaned forward and touched her friend's hand. "I'm so sorry. I'm behaving horribly. Really, I apologize. I shouldn't take out my frustration on you."

"Hey, I'm your best friend. Who better?" Beth grinned. "Why don't you tell me what's really wrong?"

"I can't explain it. You're right, I *did* know he was leaving. It shouldn't be a surprise, but it is. Maybe because I didn't see it coming. Maybe I secretly hoped he would change his mind. I'm not in love with him, he's not in love with me, but I don't want him to go. Does that make sense?"

"No."

Cindy smiled and rested her elbows on the round table. As usual, her kids were playing in the greenbelt. She could see them taking turns on a swing made from an old tire. A larger, older boy tried to push Allison out of the way. Her daughter pushed him right back and stood her ground. The boy slunk to the rear of the line.

"Allison hasn't mentioned Shelby in nearly two weeks," she said. "I finally asked about her. Allison told me that Shelby went back to her real family. I'm thrilled that Allison is doing so much better. My head tells me she would have grown up enough to let go of her imaginary friend on her own. My heart tells me it was Mike."

"What happens to Allison when Mike leaves?"

"I think she's going to miss him. We all are. I also think she's going to be fine."

Beth studied her. "So it's not Allison you're worried about."

She shook her head. "No. It's me."

"I thought it wasn't serious," her friend said. "You were supposed to be pretending."

"We were pretending. It's not real." Cindy resisted the urge to lay her head on the table. She was cranky and out of sorts and she didn't know why. Yes, of course she knew why. Mike was leaving. But why did that change anything? He'd been leaving from the moment they'd met.

"We're just friends," she said, as much for her benefit as for Beth's.

They *were* just friends. They talked and laughed and had fun. She knew she wasn't in love with him. So why was she taking this so badly? Why did she still feel that hole in her chest? It hadn't closed at all. If anything, the edges were more ragged and raw.

"That's the problem," Beth said softly. "You want to be more than friends."

Cindy opened her mouth, then closed it. She opened it again. "That's not true."

But even as she said the words, she wondered.

"Of course it is." Beth smiled. "Mike is a very good-looking man."

"You've noticed."

"Along with half the county. He's been living right next door for weeks. You've pretended to be an item. I know you've kissed him, I have witnesses."

A guilty flush stained Cindy's cheeks. Beth knew about the brief kiss witnessed in the mall. She didn't know about the half hour or so Cindy and Mike had spent on the sofa during that thunderstorm. Of course, Beth was pretty smart. She might have guessed.

"What's your point?" Cindy asked.

"You've been about as close as a man and woman can be without being lovers. Now that he's leaving, you're having regrets about not taking that final step. Considering the options, Mike is your safest bet to test yourself as a single woman."

"You're saying this is all about sex."

"Isn't everything?"

Cindy grimaced. "Not in my life. Not for a long time."

"Then you'd better do it, so you don't forget how."

"Gee, thanks for the vote of confidence."

Cindy sipped her tea. Was Beth right? Was she feeling regret for not having taken their relationship to its next level? But she and Mike didn't have a relationship. They were friends. And friends don't have sex. She'd never really even thought about it.

Liar, the voice in her head whispered. Of course she'd thought about it. There were nights she couldn't sleep for thinking about being with him, touching him and being touched. Her body had been on fire, aching, needing.

"He's not interested in me that way," she said glumly. "I don't think I turn him on."

Beth didn't say anything. Finally, Cindy looked at her friend. Beth arched her eyebrows until they nearly touched her fringed bangs. "Oh, stop it," Beth said simply. "I've seen the smoldering looks that pass between the two of you. I've seen the little knowing glances and the touches. Don't tell me you haven't played footsie a time or two."

The blush burned hotter. "We haven't really done very much."

"But you've done something."

"We've, ah, kissed."

"Did he want to do more?"

"I don't know. He didn't say anything."

Beth rolled her eyes. "Cindy Jones, you're the most unaware woman on the planet. If I didn't know for a fact that you had children, I would swear you'd never been with a man. He doesn't have to *say* anything. As for his wanting more, you know exactly what I'm talking about."

"Ah, yes, well, maybe he was a little interested."

"It's little?"

"Beth!"

Her friend grinned. "Then you have your answer."

"But he's never made a move or anything. What if it was just a normal male reaction to the situation? What if it wasn't about me specifically?"

"Then make it about you. Mike likes you. Why wouldn't he want to make love? All you have to do is let him know that *you* want to, too."

Cindy winced. "I can't do that. What on earth would I say? 'Gee, Mike, how about a roll in the hay?' What if he's not interested? Besides, it's so complicated. Where? When? And what about birth control? I haven't been on the Pill since Nelson left."

"Condoms," Beth said firmly. She took a sip of her tea and leaned forward. "This is the nineties, and you have to be sensible. Something else over-the-counter, too. Maybe that sponge thing."

"I can't do this," Cindy moaned.

"Of course you can. Besides, if you don't take care of birth control and he's not expecting the invitation, he might not be prepared. Then where would you be?"

"Don't you think it would be easier to just forget the whole thing?"

"Yes, but is that what you want?"

Cindy didn't know anymore. Part of her wanted to be with Mike. She liked him, he made her feel alive and attractive. He made her believe that her dreams were still possible. Part of her wanted to run in the opposite direction. She'd never done anything like this in her life.

"I've only ever been with Nelson," she said. "What if we've been doing it wrong?"

"Then you might as well find out now." Beth stared at her. "I don't understand. One minute you act as if you really want to do this with Mike, and the next you make me feel as if I'm pushing you into prostitution. What's going on?"

"I'm scared," Cindy admitted. "I'm afraid of what will happen if we do this, and I'm afraid of regretting it for the rest of my life if we don't. I keep telling myself that you're right. I've got to get back into circulation. I want to focus most of my attention on the children, but I have to take care of myself, too. Otherwise, when they're grown and gone, I won't have anything. It's just so hard to find the balance. And I'm terrified. What if he doesn't want me?"

Beth shook her head. "You're crazy to worry about that. You're a wonderful woman. I've seen the way Mike looks at you. Of course he wants you. What man in his right mind wouldn't?"

"Nelson didn't."

"He's dating bimbos and is hardly in his right mind. All you have to do is prepare a nice dinner. A few flowers, a tablecloth, wear a dress. He'll get the idea."

"You make it sound so simple. What if he doesn't?"

"Then take his gun and shoot him."

In spite of her concerns, Cindy laughed out loud. "A great idea, only he doesn't have a gun."

"Not to worry. You can borrow one of Darren's."

"Great. Then I'd be in prison, and I still wouldn't have been with a man."

Beth smiled. "Are the kids with Nelson this weekend?"

Cindy nodded.

"Then that's when you make your move. You won't have to worry about being disturbed. I promise not to call."

The weekend was only two days away. Could she do it? Did she want to? It seemed so calculated.

Beth rose to her feet. "I've got to get home and phone Darren."

Cindy followed her friend to the door. "You can call him from here if you want."

"No, thanks. It's going to be a very personal conversation. I'm going to tell him that I'm grateful that we're married and beg him to never leave me. I wouldn't do the single thing well."

"Tell me about it."

Beth stepped onto the front porch and paused. "You deserve this, Cindy. You've spent most of your life thinking about everyone but yourself. Take a chance. Have some fun. Mike is a good guy. He won't let you down. You don't have to fall in love. In fact, it would be easier if you didn't. Just enjoy the moment and keep it to remember later."

"That's good advice. Thanks."

She watched Beth cross the street, then circle around to her back door. She envied her friend's married state. There were negatives in all relationships, but the good often outweighed the bad. Sometimes it was boring, but right now boring sounded wonderful. She wished it could have been different.

Cindy walked back to the kitchen and carried the tea glasses to the sink. She couldn't change the past, but she could affect the future. She could make choices for the right reasons, not just because she was reacting to a situation. So what did she really want?

Mike.

The answer came swiftly and without warning. She wanted to be with him and know what it was like. Beth had been right. She needed the memories to carry with her. She liked him, she admired him. She was going to miss him when he was gone, but she wasn't in love with him. At least she'd been sensible enough to hold on to her heart.

She prayed he was interested in her that way. She was reasonably sure he wouldn't turn her down flat. After all, the few times they kissed, it had been wonderful. It would have been easy for things to get out of hand. She thought he liked her, too. It would be as simple as friends becoming lovers. Nothing more.

So she would do as Beth suggested. She would invite Mike over for dinner on Saturday night when the children were gone and she would seduce him.

Cindy had said to arrive at six, so Mike knocked on her door at 5:59. He'd brought over a bottle of wine. When a finger of guilt tickled his spine, he reminded himself he was just being neighborly and thanking Cindy for the invitation. He wasn't trying to get her drunk.

He was still smiling at the thought when she opened the back door. His mouth dropped open. He closed it quickly and stared.

"Hi," she said shyly, then stepped back to let him inside.

"Hi, yourself," he managed to say, and handed her the bottle of white wine. As she took it and moved into the kitchen, he found himself unable to look away from her long, bare legs.

He'd seen them countless times before. She wore shorts every day. So that wasn't different. But the dress was.

He found it odd that her shorts exposed more of her legs than the dress did, yet somehow a narrow skirt falling to midthigh was about a hundred times more seductive. And she'd been damned impressive in shorts.

He swallowed hard and raised his gaze. The pale peach fabric skimmed over her hips, hugged her slender waist before molding her back to her shoulders. There was a long, slim zipper from the nape of her neck down to the swell of her buttocks. His fingers itched to pull it. When she turned, he saw the sleeveless dress didn't dip especially low, but it outlined her full breasts. Wide straps left her shoulders bare.

It was a simple dress. Nothing about it screamed sex, or even seduction. But he'd never seen Cindy in a dress before. Desire burst to life, filling him with a nearly uncontrollable need and sending blood to his groin. In less than five seconds, he was obviously and painfully aroused.

"You look great," he said.

"Oh. Thanks." She touched her hair self-consciously. She'd curled it.

He moved closer. She was wearing more makeup than usual. Her eyes were dark and mysterious, her mouth full and kissable.

Slow down, Blackburne, he ordered himself. This was Cindy, his neighbor and friend. Nothing more. The dress was probably just a whim. It was Saturday night, the kids were gone and she wanted to make herself pretty. It didn't mean a thing and he would be a fool to think otherwise.

"Do you want some wine?" she asked.

"Sure." He took the corkscrew she offered and opened the bottle. While she was pouring, he noticed the kitchen table was bare. He peeked into the dining room. The large table had been set with a tablecloth and fresh flowers. There were two place settings at the far end. The dimmer switch was turned to low and there were candles waiting to be lit.

"Here." She handed him the wine.

"Thanks." He took a large swallow and nearly choked. He recovered, then coughed a couple of times.

"Are you all right?" she asked.

He cleared his throat. "Fine."

He tugged at his T-shirt. It didn't have a collar but he felt something tightening around his throat. Nerves maybe.

She sipped her wine. The kitchen was silent except for the ticking of the wall clock. The oven was on. He could smell something delicious.

"What's for dinner?" he asked.

"Beef Burgundy."

"Then I should have brought red wine."

"Oh, I have some for dinner. I thought we could have this first."

"Are you trying to get me drunk?" he teased.

Instead of laughing, Cindy looked away nervously. "Would you like to go into the living room?"

The living room? Not the family room? "Sure."

He followed her. She stopped to flip on the stereo system in the corner. The CD player had already been set. At the push of the button, soft music filled the room. He sat on the sofa, wondering if she would sit next to him. Instead, she perched nervously on the edge of the wing chair opposite. Silence stretched between them.

"It doesn't seem as hot today," she said at last. Her gaze met his, then slid away.

"I noticed. Are the kids with their dad?"

She nodded. "Nelson promised to buy them a few more things for school. Jonathan needs a jacket for when it gets colder. His is too small."

Silence again.

Mike leaned back in the couch and rested his right ankle on his opposite knee. Something was wrong. This was Cindy and they'd never had a problem talking to each other before. She was bright, funny and he enjoyed her company. Only the stranger sitting in front of him wasn't the Cindy he knew. Something had happened to her. Fear mixed with an instant need to fix whatever the problem was.

"Your hands are shaking," he said quietly. "What's wrong?"

She closed her eyes briefly and swallowed. "Nothing. Everything. Maybe you should just leave."

He lowered his foot to the ground and leaned toward her. "What? Leave? What's going on here? I thought you invited me to dinner."

"I did. I just—" She raised her gaze to his. Her irises were dark with an emotion he couldn't read. "I thought it would be easier than this. I thought—"

"What?" He set his wine on the coffee table in front of him and crossed the room. He knelt beside her and took her free hand in his. "Cindy, it's Mike. You can tell me anything. Did Nelson say something to you?"

"Of course not. We're back to him honking for the children. Everything's fine with Nelson.... It's you."

She spoke the last two words so softly, he wasn't sure he'd heard them. "Me?"

"I'm..." She snatched her hand away and glared at him. "Dammit, Mike, I'm trying to seduce you. Okay? Are you happy? You can laugh now." She set her glass on the small table to her right and clutched her fingers together.

He couldn't have been more stunned if she'd slapped him across the face. "You're trying to seduce me?"

"Stop repeating everything I say." She looked at him as if he had the IQ of a snail. "What did you think all this was?" she asked, pointing at her wineglass, then plucking at the hem of her dress. "There are candles and fresh flowers on the table."

"I noticed."

"You did? Then why didn't you say something, or better yet, do something?"

"Like rip off your clothes?"

"At least then I would have known you were interested." She rose to her feet and walked into the kitchen. Once there, she stood at the sink, with her back to the room.

"What makes you think I'm not?" he asked as he followed her.

She trembled slightly but didn't answer his question. He didn't know whether to laugh or tell her how foolish she was being. Why did she think she had to seduce him? Didn't she know how much he wanted her?

The obvious response was no. She was terrified of doing the wrong thing. Judging from the way she was acting, his suspicions that she hadn't been with anyone since her divorce had to be true. He would also guess that she hadn't been with a lot of men before her marriage. Which meant she was practically an innocent. The thought should have scared him to death. But for some macho, perverse reason, he was pleased.

"Other women have it easy," she said. "Other women seem to find men to have sex with. But not me. No, that would be too simple."

"How many men have turned you down?"

"Just you." She sighed. "Look, I'm really sorry. I shouldn't have changed the rules without checking with you first. It's not fair. I guess I just sort of hoped it would all happen naturally. If you only knew how awful all of this was."

"What's awful? The thought of making love with me?" He leaned against the doorframe.

"No, of course not. That's what I wanted. But there have been so many details to work out. I've been overwhelmed. Finding the right dress. I must have changed about fifteen times. Then I had to plan the right dinner. Something elegant, but easy to eat and prepare. And something that didn't need perfect timing. I mean, what if you'd instantly swept me off my feet? I wanted to be able to turn off the oven and not have dinner ruined."

"What else?"

She shook her head. "I didn't know which tablecloth to use. Red was too Christmassy and white was too, I don't know, weird, I guess. Like it was a wedding or something. And then there was the whole issue of birth control."

"You planned ahead?"

"Of course. I mean, what if you weren't prepared? I didn't think of that, by the way, Beth did."

"You've talked this over with her?"

"In detail." She clutched the edge of the counter so hard, her knuckles turned white. He could see the muscles in her arms tightening. "She told me to go for it."

"I always liked Beth," he murmured, more and more intrigued by this side of Cindy. She'd really thought this through. She wanted to be with him and had made it happen. He wondered if any other woman in his life had ever cared so much. He wondered if he ever had.

"What did you say?" she asked.

"Nothing. You were explaining about the birth control."

"I didn't know what to get. I haven't been on the Pill since the divorce so I needed something for me, and Beth reminded me to buy condoms. This is the nineties, and I do want to be sensible. Do you know how many kinds of condoms there are?" She spun to face him and grimaced. "About a dozen brands, all these different types, with strange descriptions. What does it all mean? I was so confused. I had to stand there reading packages, like some pervert. Plus, I had to drive clear into the city so I could find a drugstore where no one would know me.''

"I hope you bought large ones.''

"What?'' The color drained from her face. "What did you say?''

"What size box?''

"Oh.'' Some of the color returned, although most of it centered in a bright spot on her cheeks. "I don't know. The little one. I think it has three inside.''

He pushed off the doorframe and started toward her. On the way, he paused long enough to turn off the oven.

"Mike?'' She glanced around as if trying to back up. Only the kitchen sink was behind her. She was trapped.

"Only three,'' he said, stopping in front of her and lowering his mouth to hers. "That won't be nearly enough.''

Chapter Fourteen

His lips were firm. The kiss didn't last but a moment, still she felt it all the way to her toes... and her soul. Her arms hung at her sides and she curled her fingers into her palms. She wanted to touch him, she wanted to hold him and be held, only it wasn't that simple.

She broke free of the kiss, then sidestepped, slipping past him and the island, heading for the dining room. Once there, she stared at the perfectly set table and sighed. It had been a mistake from the beginning. She wasn't the seducing kind.

"You can leave now," she said.

Mike followed her. He placed his hands on her shoulders. "You can't believe that's what I want."

It was a lot easier to have this conversation without looking at him, so she continued to study the flowers she'd purchased that afternoon. "I know you wouldn't want to hurt me. We're friends, and you care about me. That caring might make you do something you'd otherwise rather not do. I'm not saying you'd have to grit your teeth and think of England, but maybe you're being pushed in a direction you don't want to go. I don't want that.''

"I'm a grown man, Cindy. I know how to say no. Right now, there's nowhere else I'd rather be. There's no one else I'd rather be with. This isn't about you seducing me, it's about me finally giving in to what I've wanted from the moment we met. Do you know what my first thought was when I was lying on my sister's sofa, more dead than alive?''

She could barely remember their meeting. Probably because he was rubbing his palms up and down her bare arms. The combination of heat and friction made it difficult to think about anything but what she was feeling. She wanted to lean back against him, against his hard, lean strength. Instead, she forced herself to murmur, "No."

"I couldn't lift my head, so all I saw were these beautiful, honey-colored thighs. I remember thinking it was very nice of God to insist angels walk around naked.''

In spite of feeling incredibly stupid and exposed, Cindy smiled. "I'm hardly an angel.''

"You're right about that.'' He turned her until she was facing him. "You're a woman, and I want to make love with you.''

His brown eyes blazed with passion. He might be able to fake the affection in his voice or the gentleness of his touch, but she doubted he would be able to invent a fire that bright without some passion to fuel it.

She wanted to believe, she needed to more than anything. Of its own accord, her hand came up and touched his jawline. The skin was smooth; he'd shaved before coming over.

She wanted to ask if he was sure. She wanted to believe it didn't matter if he wasn't. She wanted him to sweep her off her feet so she could stop thinking so much. Instead, she said, "I haven't been with anyone but Nelson. For all I know, I'm doing something terribly wrong. Promise you won't laugh?"

He smiled. "Don't you know I don't care what you do or don't do? I just want to be with you and touch you. I want to taste every part of you. I want to listen to your breathing as the promise of ecstasy makes you gasp for air. I want you to scream my name and beg for more. I want to be in you, hard and deep until you can't do anything but feel."

She stared at him, then blinked. "I'm not much of a screamer."

"That's all you got from that?"

"Well, my knees are shaking a little."

"Let's make them shake a lot."

He leaned over the table and grabbed a single white rose. After handing it to her, he bent down and picked her up in his arms. She shrieked and wrapped her arms around his neck.

"What are you doing?"

"I would have thought it was obvious."

He was strong, his hold on her secure, but she didn't like the feeling of being so out of control. "The bedroom is less than twenty feet away. I could have walked."

"That's romantic," he said, stepping into the bedroom and kicking the door closed behind him. He walked to the bed and set her down next to it. He took the rose and put it on the nightstand.

Cindy glanced around the room and winced. She'd removed the comforter and drawn back the sheets. Small unlit candles covered her dresser. There was something sheer and lacy on the counter in the bathroom, just in case.

"Call me subtle," she said miserably.

Mike didn't answer. He sat on the edge of the high mattress and grabbed her wrist. He tugged until she was forced to step between his parted thighs.

This had all been a mistake, she thought grimly. She should never have tried the seduction thing. She just didn't have the experience to be good at it. Now, glancing around at her preparations, she felt like a foolish child wishing after the moon. Or a teenager worshiping a rock star. All she needed was Mike's picture on the wall.

When the front of her thighs bumped the insides of his, Cindy returned her attention to what was going on. Mike's hands rested on her waist and he was urging her closer. The fire inside of him burned so hot she could feel the flames. They lit an answering spark within her. The spark flared to life, growing until it threatened to consume her. It burned away her doubts and questions until only need was left behind.

"Kiss me," he commanded.

She complied willingly.

His position on the bed put him slightly below eye level. She bent her head until their lips touched. She wasn't sure what she expected, maybe a wild assault, maybe cool disinterest. Instead, his lips clung to hers, touching, sharing, but not taking. She could feel the soft pressure as he moved his head slightly, fitting them together. She raised her arms and placed them around his neck. His hands settled on her back. As she moved closer, he pulled her next to him. From chest to thigh they touched.

His heat was like a sensual blanket. It swept over her shoulders wrapping her in a thick cloak of need. A tremor raced through her, then another. Yet they were only kissing, as chastely as virgin lovers who might yet be separated.

She stroked the back of his neck. His haircut was still painfully new. She could feel the first hints of stubble, then the military-short strands. She traced the shape of his ears, his jaw. Smoother skin there, but different from her own.

He shifted, splaying his legs more until her thighs settled against his groin. She could feel the hardness of him, straining against his shorts. He couldn't fake that, either. She relaxed, giving herself up to the sensual experience.

He chose the moment of her surrender to test the seam of her mouth. She parted for him instantly, anticipating the sweet taste of him and the pleasure he would bring. He didn't disappoint her. His tongue swept across hers. Shivers raced down her arms and chest, settling in her breasts. She drew in a deep breath, to bring her more in contact with him. The action didn't ease the aching she felt there, or between her legs. Even her lacy, silk bra felt scratchy and thick.

He broke the kiss, only to trail kisses across her jaw and down her neck. He licked the hollow of her throat, traced a moist path to the neckline of her dress, then moved lower still and gently bit the puckered tip of her breast.

She sucked in her breath. Through the layers of clothing, she felt the pressure of his teeth. Involuntarily, her hips arched toward him, her head arched back. Breath caught in her throat. She squeezed his shoulders, silently begging for more.

Over and over he raked his teeth against the sensitive nub. The hands at her waist held her in place. If she'd had the strength, she would have laughed. She had no plans to leave. But as she swayed slightly, unable to keep her balance under his sensual assault, she thought he might not be holding her still as much as holding her up.

She clung to him. Her fingers weaved through his silky, short hair. She cupped his head, finally urging him to taunt her other breast the same way.

His ministrations there were twice as sweet. Her legs trembled violently. Her breathing was rapid gasps. She could feel the moist heat between her thighs. She was shaken and ready for him, and they both still had their clothes on.

"Sweet Cindy," he murmured against her chest. "Tell me you like this."

"Are you kidding?" she gasped.

He raised his head and looked at her. A slow, satisfied, very male sort of smile stretched across his face. She wondered if she should be offended or at least protest the power he had over her. Before she could decide, he began pulling her zipper down and she found she didn't really care what he did, as long as he didn't ever stop.

He slipped the dress over her shoulders. It slid down easily, falling into a pool at her feet. His gaze moved from her face to her breasts, then lower. She felt it as tangibly as a touch. Her skin was both hot and cold, and she held on to his shoulders as the only solid thing in her spinning world.

"I knew you'd be this beautiful," he whispered, then kissed her collarbone.

She wanted to protest she wasn't beautiful. She was slightly over thirty, she'd had two children and she hadn't won the battle with those last couple of pounds. But he didn't seem to care and she decided not to point those facts out to him.

His fingers moved up and down her spine, creating spirals of need and anticipation. His hands slipped over her hips, then cupped her buttocks tightly. Finally, he moved down her legs to the backs of her knees, then up, repeating the journey in reverse.

Every muscle, every inch of skin longed for the brush of his fingers. As he touched her, heat flared to life, leaving tiny points of flame lit all over. He again trailed kisses down her chest, to her breasts, but this time he dipped lower. He licked the sensitive valley between her breasts, then bent his head and bit the skin over her ribs.

His breath tickled her, his hands taunted her, his mouth left her trembling and weak. It had never been like this before. Mike loved all of her, touching her everywhere, bringing her to the highest pitch of arousal she'd ever known. He didn't just stroke her breasts for a few minutes, then move his hand lower to bring her to the point of completion. He seemed to have forgotten there was a destination and was instead enjoying the journey for its own sake.

His hands moved back up her spine. Before he could taunt her again with a nibble on her side, she placed her hand under his jaw and forced him to look at her.

"Kiss me," she commanded.

"Yes, ma'am." He puckered his lips obligingly.

She smiled. "I didn't expect to laugh."

"What did you expect?"

"To feel awkward and out of place. I was afraid I was going to lie on the bed like a piece of wood, wondering how I was going to explain my lack of response."

"That doesn't say much about my technique."

"This was just a little more about my fears than your ability."

"And now?" he asked.

"I'm on fire."

She lowered her mouth to his. This time she was the one to brush his lips with hers. She learned the shape of him, then used her tongue to discover his taste. She swept over his lower lip and dipped inside, savoring the tightening of his muscles and the half-swallowed groan.

Still kissing him, she moved out of the V of his thighs, and nudged his knees together. She straddled him, bringing her waiting moistness in contact with his male need. Wiggling closer, making him writhe, she deepened the kiss, exploring all of him, learning what made him quake, what made him go still and what made that hardness flex against her.

He broke away and swore. "You're trying to make me lose control."

"Is that possible?"

"Oh, yeah. If you don't stop moving like that, you'll make me prove it."

"Thank you," she murmured. She didn't believe he was all that close to being swept over the edge, but it was wonderful to hear the words. She liked knowing she brought this strong man to the point of breaking. She wanted him to shatter, then together they would put the pieces back in place.

She kissed his jaw, tasting the faintly bitter flavor of his after-shave, then moved to his ear. She nibbled on the lobe and suckled the sensitive skin underneath. His breathing grew more rapid.

His fingers found the fastener of her bra. With practiced ease, he slipped the hooks free. She straightened slightly so the garment slid down her arms. She grabbed it and tossed it aside.

Mike stared at her breasts as if he'd never seen a naked woman before. Slowly, reverently, he cupped her. She was pale against his tanned skin. His fingers moved back and forth creating exquisite electrical sensations that arced down to her most feminine place. He lowered his head between her breasts, as if to bury himself within her. He was warm, with only the faintest hint of stubble to create delicious friction.

Her own breathing increased to match the rapid cadence of his. When his mouth closed on her nipple, she caught her breath, wondering if she'd ever felt anything so incredible in her life. His warm, damp tongue circled her, teasing her tightness until her hips began to rock against him. She gasped his name, clutching at him, begging him to never stop.

Back and forth he moved, caressing first one then the other breast. His fingers supported her, stroking her pale flesh, pushing her toward the edge of sanity.

When she thought she might slip over into madness, he wrapped his arms around her waist and gently lowered her to the bed. He rolled until he knelt between her thighs. She was stretched across the width of the mattress, her feet dangling off the side. The sheets were smooth and cool against her heated skin.

He shifted so he was lying next to her, then reached behind him for something on the nightstand. When she was able to bring her gaze into focus, she saw he was holding the rose.

"Lovely," he said, first staring at, then sniffing the pale flower. He held it close to her nose. She inhaled the sweet fragrance. Roses would forever remind her of him.

It was probably close to seven o'clock, but the sun was still bright in the sky. The pulled drapes couldn't keep out all the light. She could see him clearly, and the furniture in the room. Her nearly naked body was his to view, yet he seemed preoccupied by the rose.

"They've taken off the thorns," he said, turning the stem and studying it. "Just as well, I wouldn't want to hurt you."

With that, he brushed the flower against her throat. The petals were soft. She could smell the sweet scent and feel the faint caress against her heated skin. She arched her neck. He traced the line of her jaw, her ears, then moved down her chest to her breastbone.

The delicate petals tickled and aroused. Goose bumps dotted her skin. Mike stretched out beside her, supporting his head on one hand. With the other, he held the rose and circled her breasts. First one, around and around, moving higher to her nipple, but not touching it, then the other. Back and forth, he taunted her.

Her breathing came in gasps, then she forgot to breathe at all. At last he brushed the tip with the head of the flower. At the same moment, he brought his mouth down on her other breast. Her hips tilted, her fingers clawed at the sheet. She didn't know she could feel so much pleasure and still live.

He continued to stroke her body, dragging the rose across her belly. Every muscle quivered in anticipation. He paused to remove her panties, then trailed the flower down her legs. He tickled the soles of her feet, then moved higher, sweeping the petals across the insides of her knees and up her thighs.

She parted for him. She was damp and swollen, her woman's place aching for his touch. If she'd been able to speak, she would have begged. As it was, she could only try to survive this sensual assault, waiting for the culmination that would surely shatter her being.

He touched the rose to the damp curls. He rose and knelt between her legs. Again and again he touched her with the flower. The petals merely teased her, without bringing her the promise of release. She moved her hips up and down, silently urging him to touch her, take her. Anything.

He laughed softly. "Impatient little thing, aren't you?"

"Yes," she gasped.

He leaned forward and placed the rose on her belly. With one graceful movement, he drew his T-shirt over his head and tossed it aside. His torso was smooth and tanned, gleaming in the diffused light. She reached for him.

"Not yet," he said, lowering himself to the mattress and dropping a quick kiss on her right thigh.

His hands slipped under her legs as he grasped her buttocks, then bent closer. She screamed when he stroked his tongue against her. From the place that would bring them both release, to the tiny but engorged center of her pleasure, he tasted her. His breath was hot, his tongue sure.

She'd heard of such things, her ex-husband had even tried it once or twice, but she'd felt so awkward and exposed, she'd asked him to stop. Now the thought of Mike stopping was enough to make her sob. She could feel her body collecting itself, already prepared to explode. Her scalp tingled, the soles of her feet burned. Every point in between was alive and taut with need. Her muscles contracted and tightened, making her legs jerk and her hands clutch and release the sheet.

His tongue continued its magical ministrations, circling around, moving up and down, dipping inside, as if her flavor was a treat to be savored. He moved closer, shifting her legs over his shoulders, as if *he* needed more. She was off-balance and falling, exposed and out of control and she didn't want it to end.

But the pleasure could not be denied. Like the glory of a sunrise, it began with only a hint of light. Her muscles started to clench in a secret rhythm. Her hips rose against his mouth, her fingers clawed for support as she moaned her need.

She spoke his name, at least she tried to form the words. She tossed her head from side to side. The insistent stroking of his tongue forced her to his pace, not hers, so she hung suspended, until the last rapid flick sent her exploding into the light. She soared in a storm of ultimate pleasure as her muscles trembled in a cascade of satisfaction.

When the world had stopped spinning, she found herself cradled in Mike's arms. He stared at her intensely.

She touched his face, his cheeks, then traced his mouth.

"That was wonderful," she murmured.

"I'm glad."

"How did you do that?"

"I had great material to work with. You're very responsive."

She could feel the blush climbing, but she didn't bother to look away. After what they'd just shared, how could there be any secrets?

"I've never been that responsive before," she admitted.

"Then you *have* been doing it wrong."

She giggled. "I guess so. Thanks for showing me the right way."

"My pleasure. Anytime. And I mean that."

His eyes were dark and smoky, his expression caring. But she could feel the tension in his body. His erection pressed against her bare hip.

As she raised her head toward him, she ran her hands down his back. Even as their mouths met and tongues tangled, she stroked his coiled muscles. His skin was sleek and smooth, his strength overwhelming. Except for the scar on his leg, he was back to normal.

Even so, a slight pressure on his shoulder was all she needed to roll him onto his back. She knelt next to him and studied the breadth of him. His belly was flat, his hips narrow. The male part of him thrust up against the fabric of his shorts.

She bent over his chest and touched her tongue to his nipple. At the same moment, she placed her palm over his hardness. His response was an instant guttural cry. He cupped her face.

"You're killing me," he murmured.

"What a way to go."

His smile was slightly pained.

He sat up and kissed her. While his mouth kept hers busy, he drew off his shorts and briefs. He reached for her hand and brought it back to him. This time, instead of strained fabric, she touched bare skin. Her fingers closed around him. He drew her tongue into his mouth and sucked, matching the speed of her strokes between his thighs.

Soft skin encased the hard ridge of his desire. She explored his impressive length, then moved lower. He spread his legs, allowing her to touch him there. Flesh yielded. She cupped him gently, rubbing her fingers until he writhed against her caress and hoarsely called her name.

She lowered her mouth to his shoulder, nibbling his hot skin. He tasted salty.

"Where are they?" he asked, his breath ticking her ear.

"What?"

"The condoms."

"Oh." She raised her head and glanced at him, suddenly embarrassed. "Under the pillow."

He slid his right hand along the sheet, searched for a moment, then pulled out the small, square box.

"Did I get the right kind?" she asked, suddenly anxious. "There were so many and I didn't really know what you would want and—"

He touched his finger to her mouth. "You did great. They're fine."

She gave him one final, parting stroke, then sat back and watched him draw on the protection. She'd been afraid that moment might be awkward, but it was a caring gesture. He didn't try to persuade her otherwise, or make her feel foolish. He simply did what he had to in order to take care of her.

When he was done, she lay down next to him. He moved over her, settling between her legs. At the first touch of him against her sensitive center, her body began to clench in anticipation. She hadn't thought to experience release again, but suddenly she wanted to. Desperately.

She drew back her knees and arched her hips toward him. He pressed against her. She was so damp, he slid in easily, parting her tight flesh, sending shivers of pleasure radiating outward, like a pebble dropped in a pond. She wiggled closer. Her breasts bounced with the motion and his breath caught. She smiled slowly. She liked knowing he found her exciting.

She moved her hand and touched the trimmed stem of the rose. A few of the petals had fallen off, but most of the flower was still whole. His dark eyes met hers. She saw the need raging there, matched only by the throbbing between her legs.

She brought the flower up to his chest and stroked his skin. His muscles tensed. She did it again, this time searching out his flat nipples.

"Cindy, don't," he said tightly.

"Why not?"

"Because I won't be able to hold back."

"Maybe I don't want you to."

She brought the rose lower, dipping it into his dark curls, stroking it against the base of his organ as he withdrew, only to plunge in again.

"Two can play at this," he said, then grabbed the rose from her. He touched the head of the flower to her breasts, teasing her with a quick back and forth motion.

Now it was her turn to moan. She couldn't focus on anything but what he was doing on her chest and between her legs. Her vision blurred. She felt his muscles tense for one final assault. He groaned his denial.

"Yes," she said loudly, drawing her knees all the way to her chest and thrusting her hips toward him.

He drove deeply into her, triggering massive contractions of ecstasy. His body shook as he, too, fell into the bliss. They clung to each other until the shaking stopped and their breathing returned to normal.

Cindy lay curled next to Mike. She couldn't see the clock, but she guessed it was around ten Sunday morning. On the floor was the wooden tray she'd used to feed him while he was sick. Instead of the remains of weak soup and toast, there was an empty bottle of wine, bowls used for the beef Burgundy, and an empty pint of gourmet strawberry ice cream. She smiled when she remembered what Mike had done with that. It had been very sticky and they'd both needed a shower afterward.

He'd been right about the condoms. They used the last one just a couple of hours before. Which meant, as much as she wanted to, she really shouldn't wake him up. Although there were other ways of bringing pleasure. He had certainly proved that to her.

She turned her head so she could study his profile. His nose was straight, his mouth well formed. There was a tiny scar by his left eyebrow, probably from a childhood accident. She'd never noticed before. Probably because she'd never been this close to him before.

A lock of hair fell onto his forehead. She wanted to brush it away, but she didn't want to wake him. Instead, she scooted closer, tangling her bare legs with his.

He breathed rhythmically, sleeping without dreaming. She was too aware of herself to sleep. She could hear her heart beating, feel her skin, the tingling between her legs.

She'd expected to enjoy making love with Mike. They liked each other, they had fun together, they shared a mutual attraction. Why wouldn't it have been wonderful? So the fact that he left her breathless and trembling wasn't a surprise.

She hadn't expected to fall in love.

Cindy closed her eyes for a moment. The rush of emotions had caught her off guard. She tried to tell herself it was just a chemical reaction to the moment. Once the glow wore off, so would her feelings. But she knew the truth. Somehow in the tangle of sheets and bodies, she'd exposed her heart. She suspected she'd fallen in love with him a long time ago. Their intimacy had only forced her to acknowledge it.

She'd thought she might want to rage against the truth. But she felt calm. Knowing what she knew now, even knowing Mike was leaving, she wouldn't change anything. With him, she was alive. He reminded her she was a woman, he'd shown her she could love again. If the price of that was a broken heart, she would pay it and survive. For in time her heart would heal. The crack would always be visible, and she would never love anyone exactly as she loved Mike, but it was far better to feel the pain of loss and be among the living, than exist the way she had for the last couple of years—protecting herself from the world, merely surviving in a cocoon of fear.

Some risks were worth taking. She wouldn't try to change him. She knew the lesson well. Men leave; men like him, especially. She couldn't trap him, nor did she want to. He couldn't separate what he was from what he did and she didn't have the right to ask him to. So she would love him, and when his time was up, she would let him go.

Mike stirred against her. "Why aren't you asleep?" he asked, his voice thick with sleep.

"I was just thinking."

"'Bout what?" He pulled her closer until her head rested on his shoulder. His arm encircled her waist as her bare breasts nestled against his side.

"I was wondering if you would stay here with me until it's time for you to go back to L.A."

He opened his eyes and stared at her. His smile was slow and sexy. She felt it all the way to her toes.

"I was hoping you'd ask me. There's nothing I'd like more."

Chapter Fifteen

"You can stay just one more day," Allison said as she stared at him.

Mike dropped the T-shirt he'd been folding and gathered her close. The little girl snuggled against him. The feel of her, her scent, the trusting way she expected him to keep her safe, were all familiar to him. Too familiar. He wasn't going to be able to forget her, or any of them.

"My plane is leaving in a couple of hours."

"You can change your flight," Jonathan said.

The boy stood at the end of the bed, clutching the bedpost. He kept looking away and brushing his hand across his face.

"I've got a job to get to," Mike reminded them, releasing Allison and wondering why his chest felt so tight. "I've already delayed twice. As it is, I'm going to have to fly to Los Angeles, take care of business, then fly directly to Washington."

Cindy came into the room. She shook her head. "I told you two not to bother Mike this morning. He's on a schedule. He's already stayed as long as he can. Come on. Say goodbye, then go outside and play. All your friends are there."

Allison ran from the room. Mike stared after her for a moment. He never thought he would come to care about children, but these two had really found their way inside. School was going to be starting soon. When he was gone, he would wonder if they liked their teachers and how their classes were going. He would think about Jonathan at football games and hope Allison hadn't brought Shelby back to life.

Jonathan cleared his throat several times, then gave in to the tears. They flowed down his cheeks. Mike knelt and held out his arms. The boy flung himself into his embrace.

"I'll miss you," Mike said, his voice strangely hoarse.

"Yeah, me, too. We're still going camping, right?"

"I'll be back. I don't know when yet, but I'll call. No matter what, we're going camping."

Jonathan pushed away, then ran from the room. Before Mike could rise to his feet, Allison returned. She was carrying several large sheets of paper, the thick kind kids use for crafts. Holes had been punched along one side and yarn woven through, holding the sheets together. A strand of blond hair drifted across her cheek and she brushed it away impatiently.

"I made this," she said importantly, handing him the bundle. "It's a story about you."

She smiled and her dimples about did him in. He took the papers. On the cover, printed in fairly uneven script were the words *My Summer With Mike*. There was a drawing, done in crayon, of a man, a woman and two children. He noticed the man and the little girl were holding hands. As he turned the pages, Allison pointed out the various events to him. His arrival—she'd drawn little hearts on the bandage around his stick-figure leg—playing in the greenbelt, their trip to the mall. Other times he'd nearly forgotten about. There were two pages devoted to the campout.

On the last page, the little girl stood alone. There were x's and o's underneath her figure. "Those are hugs and kisses," she said, pointing.

Cindy stepped forward. "She made it herself. Allison even thought up the idea. She's been working on it since we found out you were leaving."

"It's beautiful," he said, touching the handmade book. "The most beautiful gift anyone has ever given me."

Allison beamed with pleasure. "Now you won't forget me."

"I could never forget you." He touched her hair, then her cheek. "I'll remember you always. I promise."

"Bye, Mike." She leaned forward and kissed his cheek, then ran from the room. A few seconds later, the back door opened and slammed shut.

He stared at the book. "I wasn't expecting anything like this. It must have taken hours."

"She really cares about you." Cindy moved close and pointed to the cover. "The best part is, she didn't put Shelby anywhere in the story. I hope that means her imaginary friend is gone for good."

He rose to his feet and laid Allison's gift on the bed. "I don't want to be responsible for her return. That concerns me."

"We'll be okay. We survived before you, we'll survive after you're gone." Her gentle smile took the sting out of her words. "Trust me, Mike. Just worry about yourself and your next job. We don't want you shot up again. You want some coffee?"

"Yeah, sure. Thanks."

She left the bedroom. He finished packing. Everything he'd brought with him, practically everything he owned could fit into two bags. There was a time he'd been proud of that. Now he wasn't so sure. He would have to carry Allison's book in his hand. He couldn't fit it into his bags without folding it and he didn't want to damage the pages. He would have to get a larger suitcase. Or leave the gift somewhere safe.

He could smell the scent of coffee, but instead of walking to the kitchen, he moved to the bedroom window. He'd spent the last week and a half with Cindy. The children had acknowledged his presence with the casual acceptance of the young. Several mornings, they'd come in early and thrown themselves on the bed. Once the children returned from their father's, he and Cindy had been careful about dressing after making love, so when Jonathan and Allison had joined them, it had been a free-for-all of tickling, jokes and laughter. He'd been part of a family.

He stared out the window at the grassy lawn beyond. The crepe myrtle was in full bloom. Come winter it would stand bare. Cindy would cut it back and then it would grow and bloom again. He would miss the blossoms. He would miss the play on the greenbelt and the awful TV cartoons. He would miss the games, the fights, the laughter and even the tears. He would miss holding Cindy and loving her. He would miss watching her shower, then making love with her quickly in the large walk-in closet, her hair still dripping down her back as she buried her face in his shoulder to muffle her moans of pleasure.

He would miss this house, and the city itself. He'd come to enjoy Sugar Land and all the suburbs had to offer. He would even miss Beth.

There was a time when the thought of his new job would have consumed him, but not today. All he could do was wish he wasn't leaving. The thought of pitting his intellect and skills against the enemy wasn't exciting. The thought of taking another bullet made him grimace. He didn't want to die. Not yet. Not when he'd found what he was looking for all his life.

If only... If only he was the right man for Cindy. If only he knew how to love and be loved. If only he had the right to stay.

"Coffee's ready," Cindy called.

Mike moved across the room. He tucked Allison's book under his arm, then collected his luggage and set it in the foyer. He'd arranged for a service to drive him to the airport. Cindy had offered, but he didn't think he could stand the goodbyes. He would rather remember her here, where she belonged.

He walked into the kitchen. Cindy was sitting at the round table. He took the chair across from her and picked up the mug she'd left there.

"When does school start?" he asked.

"In a week and a half. I go back Monday. Lesson plans and all that."

She was wearing white shorts and a green T-shirt that matched her eyes. A headband held her hair off her face. He studied her features, memorizing them for the long days ahead. He wanted to believe she would mourn him, but he knew better.

"Now that you've gotten your feet wet, you can start dating," he said.

She'd brought her cup to her lips, but she set it down untasted. "I don't think it's going to be that simple."

"You can't let Nelson win forever."

"He's not winning anymore. I don't care about him. I haven't been dressing up on the mornings he picks up the kids."

"I noticed."

She smiled sadly. "I gave him too much power. I see that now. I wanted my perfect dream, my sure thing, and I figured he was the way to get it. I've learned there are no sure things in life. We just have to take what we're given and make the best of it. My kids are happy, I'm learning to be happy. I suppose I could date if I wanted to, but not right now."

She glanced down, then quickly up again. Her eyes darkened with emotion. "I love you, Mike." She held up her hand to stop him from speaking. "Before you get all worried, I don't expect you to say anything back to me. I'm not asking for something, I just wanted you to know. At first I wasn't going to tell you, but then I realized I couldn't let you go off without saying the words. I suppose they're more for me than you. Maybe that's not fair, I don't know. But it's true. I love you." She paused. "You okay?"

"Yeah, sure." But he wasn't. He was reeling inside. Cindy had done this once before. She'd managed to bring him to his knees with just a few words. She'd learned his biggest secret, that he wasn't enough, then had blithely changed the subject.

Now she spoke of loving him. He wanted to grab her by the shoulders and shake her until she said the words again and again. At the same time, he wanted to demand she take them back. She couldn't love him. No one ever loved him. He came and went from people's lives, a brief encounter, a fond memory, but he never inspired real feelings. He couldn't.

She reached out her hand and squeezed his fingers. "I never thought I'd be willing to take that kind of risk again," she said. "You showed me that some risks are worth taking. Loving you is worth all of it. You'll be gone, and I'll miss you, but that's okay. We've had some wonderful times together. I'll always treasure them. And that's what loving is about, I think. Finding the magic in a world gone mad." She sighed. "I would love to come with you, but I can't. My life is here, with my children. Yours is somewhere else. But for this summer, we had something wonderful."

Tears glistened in her eyes. She blinked them away. "Damn. I promised myself I wouldn't cry."

"You almost never swear."

"I know. I guess I'm more upset than I thought. But I'll be fine. I promise."

He didn't want her to be fine. He wanted her to scream at him, demand that he stay. Instead, she smiled bravely.

The pain in his chest deepened. She would remain here in her world, a world full of light and love. He would return to the shadows, to his temporary jobs and a life that fit in two duffel bags.

"Cindy, I—"

Outside, a car honked.

She rose to her feet. "Your car is here. It's time to leave."

The next few minutes were a blur of hugs and goodbyes. The children ran to be with him one last time. Cindy clung to him, and kissed him feverishly. He wanted to tell her he'd changed his mind, but she was so determined to go on without him. She'd made all her plans, accepted the consequences of it all. She would be fine without him.

As the car drove away, he looked back one last time. Cindy stood with her children on either side of her. They waved. He could tell they were crying.

"Where you heading?" the driver asked.

Mike leaned back against the seat. "L.A.," he answered. "Home."

But as he spoke the word, he knew it was a lie. All he'd ever wanted, all he'd ever longed for in his life was behind him. He wondered if he would ever find his way back.

Washington, D.C., was not the place to spend August. The heat, the humidity and the tourists all conspired to make his life hell. Mike paced to the window of his small bedroom and opened it. The air conditioner clicked on in angry protest, but he ignored it. He breathed in the muggy air and closed his eyes. If he ignored the sounds, he could pretend he was in Houston again.

But he wasn't. Instead of shorts and a T-shirt, he was wearing a suit and tie. The holster strapped under his arm held a pistol. He was once again the highly trained, highly paid bodyguard.

He closed the window, but he couldn't block out the memories. He'd only been gone two weeks, but he'd already broken down and called. He'd chatted casually with Allison and Jonathan, but his conversation with Cindy had been strained. She'd started crying and told him he was making it hard to be brave. Maybe he should give them time to recover.

He'd agreed not to call again for at least a month and then only to set up a camping trip with Jonathan. That decision made, life should have been easier. But it wasn't.

He couldn't stop thinking about her. About what she'd said to him. He couldn't stop hearing her say she loved him.

He'd seen Cindy with her children. He knew how strong and constant her love was. He knew she gave unselfishly, in a way he could never have imagined. As he lay awake at night, he explored his own long-buried feelings. Since he was a child, he'd tried not to care. That was the main reason he'd left Houston. He couldn't stay with Cindy and just take. He had to be able to give something back. But he wasn't sure.

He wanted to do it right. To be the perfect husband and father. Allison and Jonathan didn't need another man walking out on them. He had to be willing to stay, no matter what. But he didn't know how to be a parent. He didn't know how to be a husband. He could barely commit long enough to be a lover.

So he honored Cindy's wish and didn't call.

But his heart ached, and the wound inside of him bled as if it would never heal. He stood by the window watching people walk by. There weren't many in this exclusive section of Georgetown. Occasionally, a mother and her children strolled by. Or maybe it was the nanny.

Allison's book lay open on his bed. He looked through it every night, studying the pictures, the wobbly lines, the misspelled words. Some people would probably laugh at her efforts and only notice the mistakes. He only saw the love.

Cindy slammed down her pen and shoved back her chair. She couldn't concentrate on anything. She walked into the kitchen and paced back and forth on the wooden floor. The house was too quiet. Allison and Jonathan were with their father. Beth and Darren had taken their children to Galveston for the weekend. The neighborhood was strangely silent. She felt as if she were the only person left alive.

She wanted to jump out of her skin.

Cindy rubbed her hands up and down her arms. She was hot and cold at the same time. If she'd been able to delude herself, she would have tried to explain away her symptoms as some kind of flu. But it was simpler than that—and more deadly. She missed Mike.

It had seemed so easy when he was leaving. Loving him had been the right thing to do. It was worth the price she would pay later. Cheap talk while she was still able to see him and hold him and make love to him. Now that she was alone, all she could feel was empty. It was worse than when Nelson left. At least then she'd had her anger to give her energy.

She wanted Mike back. She wanted him to stay with her and be a part of her life. She wanted to wake up next to him and grow old with him. She wanted him to love her back.

She paused by the sink and clutched the cool tiles. That was the killer. He didn't love her. Oh, he probably cared a lot, maybe more than he'd ever cared for anyone. But she knew men like him. Men who came and went on a whim. It wasn't possible for them to put down roots. And even if Mike wanted to, he didn't believe he could. Somehow, somewhere, someone had convinced him he wasn't worth it. So he would never saddle her with what he would consider a flawed man.

She'd let him go because it was the right thing to do. Letting him go had been—

She raised her head and stared out the window. Okay. She was alone. It was time to be completely honest with herself. Letting him go had been stupid. About the stupidest thing she'd ever done. If she lived to be a thousand, she would never find a man as wonderful, as caring, as loving as Mike. And she'd let him walk out of her life. Why?

Cindy drew in a deep breath. The answer to the question floated in her brain for several moments before all the parts connected into a thought she could understand. She'd let him go because the pain of leaving was something she understood. That rejection had happened to her many times before. Demanding what she wanted, what was right for him and for her kids was so much harder. It was uncharted ground. She'd retreated to the familiar and in doing so, had lost him.

She loved him with all her heart, and if she was honest with herself, she believed he loved her back. Look at all he'd done for her. Every action had spoken of caring. Mike was a man who showed his feelings by what he did, not what he said. In time, he would have found the words. But instead of being brave enough to fight for him, she'd passively let him walk out of her life.

She crossed the kitchen in three quick steps. After fumbling through her small personal phone directory, she punched in several numbers, pausing to double-check and get them right. The connection took a few seconds. There was a bit of static, then a sleepy, "'Llo?"

"Grace?"

"Cindy? Is that you?" She heard rustling bedclothes. "What's wrong?"

"Nothing." She glanced at the clock, then added on the extra hours. "Sorry, it's the middle of the night there, isn't it? I didn't mean to wake you."

"It's okay. Are you all right?"

"Yes. No. I need to know how to get hold of Mike. He's gone and I don't have the number."

"You want to phone Mike? Why?"

"I just have to find him." She drew in a deep breath and clutched the receiver tightly. "If you must know, I love him. I let him walk out of my life because I'm a fool. I know he cares about me and the children, but he's afraid to take that last step. I've got to find him and tell him to come home to us before something terrible happens. He's on a job. What if he gets shot again? Oh, Grace, I was so brave when he left. I made him think I was going to be fine. I'm not fine. I'm a wreck. I have to tell him how much I need him."

"Oh, Cindy, this is wonderful." Grace sniffed as if she was crying, too. "I don't know where he is, but I'll find him for you. I swear I will."

Donovan raised one dark eyebrow. "You're walking away from a great job."

"Maybe," Mike said. "I'll admit the pay is good, but I don't need to go up against a bullet again."

His replacement smiled. "Don't worry. I'll get the bastard."

"You do that."

The younger man strolled out of the room. Mike watched him go, then shook his head. He'd been like that once. Eager, willing to risk it all. But it wasn't that simple anymore. He had something to live for. Three somethings. Four, if he could convince Cindy to have a baby.

He glanced around the room one last time, then picked up his luggage. He'd replaced one of his duffel bags with a large hard-sided suitcase. Allison's book fit neatly in the bottom. It meant he would have to check his luggage. He wouldn't be able to just walk away when he reached his destination. It was going to be a change, but that's what he wanted.

He was nearly out the door when the phone rang. He paused, not wanting to answer it, but what if it was Cindy? Even as he crossed to the instrument, he reminded himself she didn't have his number.

"Hello?"

"You haven't been all that easy to track down, mister."

"Grace, how'd you find me?"

"I have my ways."

"How are you?"

"Don't change the subject or try to sweet-talk me. Cindy misses you terribly. I want to know what you've done to my best friend."

"I fell in love with her."

There was a pause, then Grace laughed. "About time, big brother."

He stopped long enough to buy a four-door sedan, in dark blue. The rich, leather interior would take a beating from the kids' toys and sports equipment, but he didn't care. He was back.

He exited the highway and turned left into Sugar Land. The streets and stores were familiar to him. A week from Monday he would join the commuters making their way into the city. He would only have to go halfway there. His new job, training oil executives to ward off terrorist attacks and kidnappings, was about five miles from Cindy's house. The pay was good, the hours better. He got off every day at five.

He turned left, finally pulling to a stop in front of the middle school. The two-story brick building was exactly as he remembered it from the times he'd driven past. Up the road was the grocery store, and back the other way, the country club. He knew this small community and the residents. He wondered how disappointed the women would be now that he wasn't a bodyguard anymore. If he had his way, he wasn't going to be single much longer, either.

He found the administration office and got directions to Cindy's classroom. The door was solid wood, except for a window in the top half. He stood there looking at her.

She was wearing a skirt and blouse. Low heels made her perfect legs look even more curvy. As he watched her explaining an equation on the blackboard, he felt the wound in his chest begin to heal. How could he have ever thought of leaving her? This was where he belonged.

After a few minutes, she glanced up and noticed him. Her face paled. She said something to her class, then crossed the floor and stepped into the hall. The door closed behind her.

"Mike?" she said as if she couldn't believe it was him.

"Oh, God, I've missed you." He wrapped his arms around her. They clung to each other. Her body melted against his.

"What are you doing here?" she asked, her voice thick with emotion. "I never thought I'd see you again."

"I said I'd come back to take Jonathan camping."

"Oh. Is that why you're here?"

"No." He released her. She ducked her head, but he touched his finger to her chin, forcing her to look at him. Tears swam in her green eyes. "I came back for you, Cindy Jones. I couldn't think about anything but you. I did a lousy job, and I couldn't see myself getting any better, so I quit." He stared at her intently. "I'm not very good at relationships. I've never had one before. Not like this. So you'll have to tell me when I do something wrong. I'll try my damnedest to be the kind of man you and the kids need. I just want to be with the three of you forever. I love you."

She was staring at him, openmouthed. He swallowed. "That is, if you want me."

"Want you? I love you. I shouldn't have let you go." She leaned against him and sighed. "Are you really here? Is this happening?"

"Yes. All of it." He touched her hair. "I bought a car."

"What?"

"It's kind of big, but it will hold all the kids. There's even room for a car seat if we, ah, you know." He had to clear his throat. "I got another job. Here in town. I've got four weeks' paid vacation, benefits and I get off work at five every day."

"You want a baby, too? I'd love another child." The joy in her smile nearly blinded him. "I can't believe this is happening. You have a job here?"

"Believe it." He took her hands in his. "Cindy, will you marry me?"

Her green eyes burned bright with love. She squeezed his fingers. "You don't have to do all this for me. Just having you back is enough."

"I want to do it right. I want to get a barbecue and learn how to cook ribs. I want to mow the lawn, go to swim meets and make love with my wife every Saturday morning."

"I hope we make love more than that," she teased.

"You have to ask?"

She touched his face. "These are big changes for you. We don't have to do them all at once. Maybe we should have a trial run and see if you can stand living in the suburbs."

He shook his head. "I'm going to marry you. I've been in the suburbs, and I think they might grow on me. Besides, I can't just move in with you."

"Why not?"

He turned her slowly in a circle. Her class was plastered against the door window, staring at them. Administration office personnel stood at the end of the hall. Several teachers had come out of their rooms and were also watching them. "That's why."

"Oh, my."

"Yeah. I have your reputation to think of. What would the neighbors think if we lived together? It would cause a scandal. Besides, you're not getting away from me again. So we're getting married."

"If you insist," she said, reaching up and pressing her mouth against his. She pulled back slightly and grinned. "I can't wait to tell the kids and everyone. They're going to think it's wonderful."

"So do I," Mike said, wrapping his arms around her. "So do I."

* * * * *

COMING NEXT MONTH

MORGAN'S MERCENARIES:
LOVE AND DANGER

by Lindsay McKenna

Four missions—save Morgan Trayhern and each member of his family. Four men—each battling danger. Would rescuing their comrade help them discover the glory of love?

Watch for the next exciting title in this new series from Lindsay McKenna:

MORGAN'S MARRIAGE (SE #1005)

After a dramatic rescue, amnesia now robbed Morgan Trayhern of any recollection of his loved ones. But Laura Trayhern was determined to help bring her husband's memory back—and hoped they could renew the vows of love they'd once made to each other.

Don't miss the emotional conclusion to this series from Lindsay McKenna and Silhouette Special Edition!

New Year's Resolution: Don't fall in love!

Little Amy Walsh wanted a daddy. And she had picked out single dad Travis Keegan as the perfect match for her widowed mom, Veronica—two people who wanted no part of romance in the coming year. But that was *before* Amy's relentless matchmaking efforts....

Don't miss
NEW YEAR'S DADDY
by Lisa Jackson
(SE #1004, January)

It's a HOLIDAY ELOPEMENT—the season of loving gets an added boost with a wedding. Catch the holiday spirit and the bouquet! Only from Silhouette Special Edition!

FRIENDS, LOVERS...AND BABIES
by Joan Elliott Pickart

Joan Elliott Pickart brings her own special brand of humor to these heartwarming tales of the MacAllister men. For these three carefree bachelors, predicting the particulars of the MacAllister babies is much easier than predicting when wedding bells will sound!

In February 1996, the most romantic month of the year. Ryan MacAllister discovers true love—and fatherhood—in *Friends, Lovers...and Babies,* book two of THE BABY BET.

And in April 1996, Silhouette Special Edition brings you the final story of love and surprise from the MacAllister clan.

BABBET2

Silhouette

SPECIAL EDITION ™

Special Edition is proud to announce the arrival of our newest edition

THAT'S MY BABY!

Beginning in February, and due to arrive every other month, THAT'S MY BABY! will feature stories of bringing up baby—and finding romance and love—by some of your favorite authors:

Sherryl Woods
Laurie Paige
Barbara Faith

Plus many more!

Don't miss the wonderful stories THAT'S MY BABY! will deliver. Sometimes bringing up baby can bring surprises...and showers of love! Only from Silhouette Special Edition!

TMB-G

Silhouette
SPECIAL EDITION
THE FAMILY ™ WAY

Gina Ferris Wilkins

When their beloved Gram begins to play matchmaker,
four cousins find love in the new series by
Gina Ferris Wilkins! Meet Adam—and the rest of his
family—in Book Three,

A HOME FOR ADAM
(SE #980, September)

Dr. Adam Stone's rest and solitude were interrupted
when a very pregnant woman appeared on his
doorstep. He helped bring Jenny Newcomb's daughter into the world—and from the moment he looked at
mother and child, he wondered if they could provide
the love he needed....

Don't miss the warm and wonderful THE FAMILY WAY
series! Only from Gina Ferris Wilkins, and
Silhouette Special Edition!
